"They didn't even bring any spaceships of their own to ...

"Indeed," replied the ... , I would have all of you understand, represent any great failing on the part of the Elders. You humans generated an interest in going to the stars which the Elders never developed. But you have never—or at least very seldom—thought about traveling to other alternative universes.

"In any event," continued the giant insect, "upon departing the Solar System, the Predecessors of the Elders seem to have deliberately left behind the secret of their faster-than-light 'Virtual Drive.'"

"It is meant," declared a voice they all recognized, "as the inheritance of whatever Successor species eventually finds it."

Five beings turned as one to face the tent door.

Through it slithered a glistening twelve-foot snake which spoke with the voice of the Proprietor!

▽

CONVERSE AND CONFLICT

Also by L. Neil Smith

CONTACT AND COMMUNE

Published by
POPULAR LIBRARY

CONVERSE AND CONFLICT

L. NEIL SMITH

POPULAR LIBRARY

An Imprint of Warner Books, Inc.

A Warner Communications Company

POPULAR LIBRARY EDITION

Copyright © 1990 by L. Neil Smith
All rights reserved.

Cover illustration by Wayne Barlowe

Popular Library books are published by
Warner Books, Inc.
666 Fifth Avenue
New York, N.Y. 10103

A Warner Communications Company

Printed in the United States of America

First Printing: June, 1990

10 9 8 7 6 5 4 3 2 1

This Book is Dedicated to Bob and Laura Arbury, Dave Blackmon, Ken Flurchick, Michael Szesny, and Kitty Woldow, for reasons that will be obvious to each of them when they recall the summer of '88.

Table of Contents

Prologue
Cold Fusion

"Enter, Comrade Admiral! Sit! Have some vodka!"

Nikola Deshovich lifted a hairy hand, the stub of a cigar protruding between its first and second fingers. Inboard the *Lavrenti Pavlovich Beria*, he alone smoked, for who had the power to forbid it? Known as "the Banker" for his habit of settling old political debts "with interest," he was the absolute and undisputed master of the Soviet Union—and more recently of the United World Soviet, as well. The air in the little room was blue and foul.

To hear Deshovich speak, thought Admiral Ghasil Mubakkir, was a sensual delight. He had a way of spacing words, pausing at unexpected intervals, that compelled. His voice was deep, with a hint of velvet that massaged and reassured, although it could turn cold and toneless when that served. Now he indicated the opposite bulkhead where a chair could be unfolded. He occupied another which would have been hideously uncomfortable beneath his great mass under ordinary circumstances. With an inward sigh, Mubakkir reflected that these were hardly ordinary circumstances. He dropped an unreturned salute and attempted to relax from the reflexive military posture he'd assumed on knocking at the door of the one real passenger accommodation inboard the *Beria*, the cabin which, by rights, should have been his own.

"No vodka, thank you, sir."

The cabin wasn't spacious, nor particularly cramped. Deshovich appeared to fill it (the admiral didn't have to

1

guess his mass at two hundred kilos; it was on the manifest), leaving room for two chairs, a small table on which a bottle stood with two glasses, and the cot, covered by a rumpled quilt, which had served as an acceleration couch during a liftoff that must have seemed unendurable. Mubakkir conspicuously kept his gaze from lingering over a curvaceous form the bedclothes failed to conceal, apparently still fast asleep. He unfolded a chair because it was easier than refusing and sat, trying not to crease his snow white uniform trousers. He was known throughout the services for remaining crisp and spotless even in the heat of maneuvers in which others found themselves soot blackened, oil stained, and streaked with sweat. It set an example for subordinates who whispered that if the Old Man were ever wounded in battle, he'd somehow manage to bleed neatly.

"I'm on duty."

The fact was that he never availed himself of luxuries within easy reach of his rank. As a rising young Third World officer in the corrupt navy of a decaying world power, it had given him an edge on the competition. It had nothing to do with his religious background. Mubakkir had one God, Marx, and at the moment Deshovich was His prophet. The admiral was no saint; he merely felt he was lucky that his one vice, in which he indulged himself fully, was also his solemn obligation: command.

"Don't mind if I do," Deshovich laughed heartily. Despite his great size, he conveyed an impression of fastidious dexterity. His thick hair and gray-shot beard were trim. His black silk pajama suit was cut as nicely as the admiral's. "Until my own duty recommences, I'm simply cargo," he laid a hand across his middle, "bereft that I won't experience the weightlessness I was rather looking forward to. Well, leaving nine-tenths of Earth's gravity behind represents considerable relief in itself. It also serves to keep things—bottles, glasses, one's skeletal calcium—in their places. I'm grateful to our Bureau of Suppressed Technologies that, instead of the better part of a year, the voyage will last only days. To think America might have had cold fusion sixty years ago!''

''It gored too many well-fed oxen,'' Mubakkir nodded, ''petrol cartels and power collectives, so they buried it and discredited its discoverers.''

''So much for free enterprise!'' The Banker laughed again. ''Is this what gravity will be like when we arrive? Tell me, Comrade Admiral, what have you learned of events at our destination?''

Mubakkir watched him pour four fingers of Stolichnaya, sprinkling black pepper over the liquid surface. The gesture was pure affectation; he was too young to have lived through the harsh times when it was needed to counter the poisons of inept distillery, but it served a purpose, just like the admiral's sparkling uniforms, warning underlings and rivals that, despite generations of *détente*, *glasnost*, and *perestroika*, Deshovich's guiding spirit, summonable at need, was that of a Djugashvili.

''We lack detail, sir. According to reports from the mission commander, an AeroSpace Force Brigadier named Gutierrez, the interplanetary expedition of the American Soviet Socialist Republic arrived at the asteroid 5023 Eris less than a week ago and has already suffered five fatalities in an original complement of only forty-two. A Russian national on loan from Moscow University appears to have been murdered.''

Deshovich took a sip of vodka, puffed his cigar only to find that it had gone out, relit it, and took another drink. ''Careless of Gutierrez. Still, I suppose these things are to be expected under the circumstances. . . .''

''Yes, sir: humans in space the first time in half a century, in three refitted eighty-year-old NASA shuttles . . .''

''*Howard M. Metzenbaum*, *James C. Wright*, and *Daniel P. Moynihan*, for three obscure martyrs of the American Sovietization.'' He shook his head. ''No, Admiral, I meant the property claim being made by these aliens—''

''Not aliens, sir.'' Mubakkir shifted on his chair uneasily.

"Molluscs, referred to politely as 'the Elders,' from another version of Earth, who came to the asteroid across lines of alternative probability. Imagine a long-tentacled squid in an automobile-sized snail shell—"

"*You* imagine it!" Deshovich raised a hand, palm out. "I haven't had breakfast yet."

Mubakkir blinked. "5023 Eris is carbonaceous chondrite, sir, promising for settlement. The Elders have equipped it with an atmosphere under a sort of canopy supported by giant treelike plants. The reports mention thick vegetation and abundant moisture."

"The sort of things giant snails might like," Deshovich grunted.

"Yes, sir. In any case, one of them was killed, too, on illegal orders from the American KGB, by a Marine major later brevetted to full colonel in *our* KGB to investigate the very murder she'd committed!"

Deshovich shook his head, half-amused, half-disgusted. "I've spoken with Intelligence about that. Some of them are now investigating the Tunguska region of Siberia for pieces of an alien spacecraft which may have exploded there in 1908."

Mubakkir suppressed a rueful grin. Elsewhere, he knew, heads had rolled rather more dramatically for issuing that illegal order. One purpose of this mission was to mend fences with these living fossils who, despite a quaint, incomprehensible ethical philosophy, had brought along thermonuclear matter-energy converters like kerosene lanterns to a picnic. An economically crippled United World Soviet needed technology like that—and anything else its leader could pry loose.

Sensing the admiral's distraction, Deshovich cleared his throat. "You've taken over from American Mission Control?"

Mubakkir nodded. "We're timing our replies so the expedition will think we're transmitting from Earth."

"Excellent. By the way, Admiral, if you wished to

dispose of something aboard this vessel, how would you go about it?''

''Sir?'' Mubakkir tried not to look surprised at the change of subject. ''An airlock, I suppose. At this acceleration, it would—''

''Airlock, you say?'' With a broad hand, Deshovich reached over to flip back a corner of the duvet. Beneath it, features obscured by a fall of dark, silky, waist-length hair, lay the naked body of a young girl, flesh white with the pallor of death. Between her hips and knees the sheet was soaked with blood. ''My secretary seems to have had an accident during dictation. Get her out and have this cleaned up.

''And summon me another girl from the pool. A blond this time, I think.''

I
Absent Friends

Less than a week, he thought, *and already five graves*.

Lieutenant Colonel Juan Sebastiano stared grimly at the low mounds of carbonaceous soil covering the earthly remains (if "earthly" was the word) of five members of the expedition of which he suddenly found himself second in command, that of the American Soviet Socialist Republic to the asteroid 5023 Eris. The only thing missing to set the appropriate tone, he thought, was the oppressive drizzly overcast of their first couple of days here.

Their hosts, however, the giant molluscs who claimed this place by virtue of previous occupancy, had adjusted its artificial atmosphere. Rain would now fall at night when it wouldn't represent an inconvenience. At present, without producing shadows, a diffuse golden glow seeped through overhead to tumble down a series of small craters overlapping in broad natural stairsteps across the newly spaded ground.

Lush undergrowth surrounded the forlorn gravesite beneath sequoia-dwarfing plants that supported the world-enveloping organic canopy. "Super kudzu," Professor Kamanov had called them. The asteroid was covered, more densely than any closeups of the Moon or Mars Sebastiano had studied during training, with impact features of all sizes, cloaked in vegetation. They textured the land in unpredictable ways. General Gutierrez had begun using a thesaurus to find synonyms for "hill" and "ridge" for reports that would probably never be transmitted back to Earth now.

Poor old Kamanov.

Sebastiano drew on an unfiltered, unsanctioned cigarette which his boss's son, Second Lieutenant Danny Gutierrez, had smuggled inboard the *Metzenbaum*, one of three old NASA shuttles that had borne them hundreds of millions of klicks deeper into space than Man had ever ventured before. He guessed that made them all heroes of some kind. To the ASSR they were nothing more than expendable veterans of numerous small conflicts it was unpragmatic to commemorate. Or they were incompetent (or overcompetent) bureaucrats, or officers who couldn't keep their opinions to themselves, or enlisted personnel who insisted on remaining individuals—in short, non–team players, well worth disposing of even if they discovered nothing of value out here among the debris of a broken planet.

Or a planet that had never been.

A blue-gray wisp from the cigarette's front end irritated the colonel's nose. It was nothing, he supposed, to what the back end must be doing to his lungs. He'd given up the habit years ago, in fighter school. Since then he'd struggled for physical and mental survival through three brushfire wars, each bloodier, each emptier of meaning and purpose, than the last. But it had taken these five incredibly stupid, wasteful deaths—and certain attendant complications that had only aggravated tensions over conflicting claims to the asteroid—to get him started smoking again.

Kamanov occupied the grave on the far left. Like most members of the expedition, Sebastiano had grown fond of the old man over the year-long voyage and the longer training period before that. More in love with life and fuller of it than anyone the colonel had ever known, as mission geologist Kamanov had been among a small group on loan from the Russians. This was billed as a cooperative venture, after all, on behalf of a new and fragile United World Soviet held together at this moment in history by wishful thinking and gunship diplomacy. He'd been horribly murdered to make a political point that seemed more obscure to Sebastiano with every day that passed.

In the next grave lay Delbert Roo, carried on the expedition roster as a mining equipment operator, but in reality a KGB enforcer who'd drawn his last breath without learning (except in that last astonished fraction of a second) that there were some individuals he wasn't free to terrorize and torture as he wished.

Broward Hake, in the third grave, had been Roo's colleague in thuggery. He was dead due to a regrettable mistake, the .41 caliber pistol bullet that had finished him having been intended for someone else.

Colonel Vivian Richardson, in the fourth grave, had been the mission's original vice-commander and possibly an agent of the Russian KGB—as opposed to the American KGB which was openly represented on the expedition. She'd died the same as Hake, or at least by a projectile of the same caliber, suggesting to Sebastiano that there might be some justice in an otherwise uncaring universe, since she'd been the one who'd shot Hake.

At the end of the dismal row was a fifth grave, that of Marine Corps Major Estrellita Reille y Sanchez, a lovely redhead—lovely no longer—who'd started the whole mess against her own better judgment, having been given certain unpleasant tasks to perform whether she wanted them or not. Her life had been choked off in its twenty-eighth year as Kamanov's had in his sixty-eighth. In Sebastiano's opinion it had been too soon for either of them. Life was too short, no matter how long it lasted.

There should have been a sixth grave for Semlohcolresh, that irascible old slug. (Technically, he and his fellow monsters—make that "sapient living fossils"—were descendants of Silurian era nautiloids.) There might have been, too, if his culture's burial customs were anything like humanity's. Sebastiano didn't know what the nautiloids, with their exotic philosophy, considered decent under the circumstances, but in any case it was academic. The squidlike body of Semlohcolresh, along with its Volkswagen-sized shell, had been dissolved into its constituent nuclei in the matter-energy converter his people—and the nightmare menagerie they'd brought with them across cosmic lines of probability from countless versions of Earth—used to power their colony here.

"Colonel?"

Behind him Sebastiano heard a footfall, then the polite, apologetic cough of someone he outranked. It was Major (formerly Lieutenant Commander) Jesus Ortiz, newly appointed captain of the *Wright*. Sebastiano dropped his cigarette, slowly pivoted his bootsole on it, and turned from contemplation of the graves.

"What's up, Maje?"

"Could you come back to the *Moynihan*, Juan, ASAP? Mission Control's on the horn and they don't sound happy. The general's asking for you. He looks worried."

The Banker! Sebastiano shuddered. *It can only be the Banker!*

But he nodded and, following the major, headed in the direction of the campsite where the shuttles rested in a triangle which, more and more, seemed to him like the circled wagons of frightened pioneers in hostile Indian territory.

II
Laika

The Banker! The idea sent chills down the spine of General Horatio Gutierrez. *It could only be the Banker!* "I don't know, Juan," he shrugged, attempting to appear calm, "they just said have all hands stand by for a message from 'the highest authority.'"

Surrounded by an array of switches and lights bewildering to anyone who lacked the training they shared, he watched Sebastiano lower himself into the lefthand seat, a position the colonel normally occupied aboard the *Metzenbaum*. This was the *Moynihan*, flagship of the expedition. Sebastiano adjusted the microphone tube of his Snoopy Cap, the communications carrier he'd just jammed over his head.

Juan looked like a daredevil astronaut, Gutierrez always thought. His teeth shone white against a dark complexion. Almost as tall sitting down as the general was standing up, he sported a diabolical strip of Castillian beard and a nose that was pure Aztec. The confident movement of his slender fingers across the controls spoke of a competence rare these days in America or anywhere in the world—except, it was rumored, Switzerland, South Africa, and maybe China. Who could ever tell about China?

Standing behind him, Gutierrez twisted his neck for the fifth time in as many minutes to peer at the portside audio panel, waiting, he realized sourly, like the little dog to hear his master's voice. Through a window he saw a glint of copper rising in a graceful arc from one of many antenna penetrations in the fuselage to a great pseudotree that supported, and finally became, the atmospheric canopy a kilometer overhead. It would be some time, however, before his chance came to listen or to speak, and even then, given the vast distance involved, no real conversation with Earth would be possible. From Earth's viewpoint, it was an ideal situation: Gutierrez and his people were in a position only to receive orders and acknowledge them.

Three hundred million kilometers, he thought. At the moment, nearly two astronomical units lay between Earth and the asteroid, meaning it was twice as far from humanity's home to 5023 Eris as it was from Earth to the Sun. At a walking pace of six and a half klicks an hour, he figured, stabbing buttons on his calculator watch as if literally killing time, it was a stroll of 5,308 years, almost the totality of written history—*human* history; from now on he'd have to add that modifier. Running at top speed, the fastest man alive might have shortened it to 1,416 years (the span since Moslems had begun praying toward Mecca), had he been able to keep the pace and had there been someplace to set his feet in all that vast black emptiness. An auto cruising at one hundred kilometers per hour might have made the trip in three and a half centuries, an airliner, ten times fleeter, in only thirty-five years.

Three hundred million kilometers. Lightlike energies crossed the vacuum at three hundred thousand klicks a second. It would require seventeen minutes for signals to arrive at the asteroid from their point of origin and seventeen more for an answer to be heard on Earth, making it an astonishing thirty-four minutes from "How are you?" to "I'm fine, thanks, and yourself?"

Three hundred million kilometers. In a sense, time and place had chosen one another. This was as close as Earth and Eris ever got. The two bodies whirled about the Solar primary at their own individual velocities, like hands on an analog clock. Given that model, it was now 3:15. Before now, and in time to come, when they were on opposite sides of the giant fusion furnace at the center of the System, the distance would double to four units and it would be a quarter past nine. Had this been the case at present, another target would have been selected for the ASSR's first (and now probably last) interplanetary mission, and things might have turned out rather differently.

For the tenth time, Gutierrez checked the row of toggles on the audio panel, making sure the system would relay signals to speakers throughout the ship, to others set up in the campsite outside, and to the remaining pair of shuttles. His attention was focused forward but he could hear, and feel through the deck, the flight area filling up with curious and worried comrades.

In a corner by the life support controls, Arthur Empleado of the American KGB kept to himself. Or maybe others were avoiding him. Dark as Sebastiano, older, not nearly as well muscled nor as tall, he'd begun to acquire a paunch. In another five years his widow's peak would disappear and he'd be bald. The general thought he looked naked deprived of the goons who'd been his shadows the past year. One of them didn't want any more to do with him. Two were dead. A third nursed a ruined knee inboard one of the other spacecraft which housed a makeshift infirmary.

Gutierrez looked for Rosalind Nguyen in what was becoming a crowd. The *Moynihan*'s command deck wasn't roomy. It was like a party in a shoebox. Even "Rubber Chicken" Alvarez, cook, garbage disposer, and self-appointed clown, was here. Gutierrez wondered whether his cooking or his practical jokes had won him the nickname. Where was Rosalind? It struck him that with Estrellita gone, the Vietnamese physician was the best-looking woman on 5023 Eris. The unbidden thought made him feel guilty, not only toward his wife of thirty years (that always happened when he thought of other women), but toward poor, dead Reille y Sanchez. For refuge he resumed his earlier ruminations, reflecting that the interceptor he'd waged war in might have brought him here in a mere eleven years, had it been able to carry enough fuel for the voyage and had there been something for its engines to breathe. As it was, the ancient shuttles they'd inherited, another order of magnitude faster, had managed the task for him and the others in a little over a year.

"General?" Technical Sergeant Toya Pulaski, amateur paleobiologist (and as it turned out, they'd needed one), handed him a cup. An odd girl, nervous and plain, she'd figured out what was happening here before any of the beings who knew had gotten around to explaining it. The coffee was a gift from those who were at once their hosts and the source of half their troubles. The other half originated with the voices they were waiting to hear on the radio.

"Thanks, Toya. Hullo, Eichra Oren, Sam." Gutierrez sipped coffee. He'd become aware that beside him stood the only human here who hadn't arrived in one of the shuttles, one of an unknown number of nonnautiloids the Elders had brought with them from various alternative realities. At his knee, as usual, sat a large, white, shaggy dog, its black-lipped grin resembling a Samoyed's.

Eichra Oren was an "Appropriated Person," descended from those rescued by the Elders (or kidnapped, depending on who told it) across lines of probability some fifteen thousand years ago when a disastrous magnetic pole-shift had turned Antarctica into the frozen waste it was today, spawning legends like that of Atlantis. Not a large man (something about the way he carried himself made up for that), he practiced an almost magical martial art which resembled interpretive dancing and produced truly horrifying results. He'd killed Roo in self-defense with no more than a fingertip applied gently to the forehead. Fair-skinned with medium-length yellow hair and light-colored eyes, he appeared between twenty-five and thirty years old. Born into a culture gone from Earth for fifteen millennia, he chose to wear faded denims and Hawaiian shirts among his ship-suited fellow humans, perhaps to make his civilian status as plain to them as possible. He was inboard the *Moynihan* today as an observer for the Elders, although he'd first come to the asteroid as a kind of policeman or judge.

At last a voice issued from the radio, filtered and hissing from a voyage across unimaginable distance, yet still carrying the precise, compelling tones for which its owner was famous: *"Official message to officers and crew of the interplanetary expedition of the American Soviet Socialist Republic."*

"The Banker!" The hoarse whisper issued from an aft crewstation. It must be Empleado, Gutierrez thought, if only because of his penchant for stating the obvious. Eichra Oren looked a question.

"Nikola Deshovich," Gutierrez told him, "the real power now on Earth."

"Under him," somebody quipped, "the KGB compounds your fractures daily."

Deshovich was going on: "*Those who have been your national leaders, now retired in the light of events on Eris 5023, are enjoying a well-deserved rest in contemplative isolation.*"

Eichra Oren raised an eyebrow. "Meaning they've been jailed or killed?"

Gutierrez nodded. "Because of what Deshovich and his cronies regard as their bungling of the situation here."

The man shook his head. "All that, from just 'in the light of.'"

The general put a finger to his lips. "There's more."

"*. . . while suitable candidates for their replacement are sought. I, as Chief Executive, have undertaken to fulfill their responsibilities, as much for the sake of the people of the American Soviet Socialist Republic as for the United World Soviet as a whole.*"

Sebastiano wrenched around in his seat, looking up as if to say, *Here comes the real message!* Gutierrez gave him the same librarian's signal he'd given Eichra Oren and took another drink of coffee.

"*My first task must be to deal with counterrevolutionary contamination of Marxist thought arising from your incautious fraternization with certain indigenous reactionary elements, which now threatens to impair our long-held mutual goal of an enlightened, ideologically unified Cosmic Collective.*"

So the old dream, a System-wide Soviet, was still alive. Gutierrez shook his head. If not for "incautious fraternization," they'd all have starved or suffocated by now. Much of the expedition's equipment, as well as many of its personnel, had proven less than adequate.

Sebastiano grinned openly at Eichra Oren. "Bad enough your Elders are individualists," he offered, "they're capitalists, too!"

Eichra Oren shrugged as if to say it wasn't his fault, although everyone knew he shared the nautiloids' peculiar philosophy. Seeing it enforced (not quite the same as enforcing it) was his profession.

Unaware of Sebastiano's commentary, Deshovich went on: "... *unless a way can be devised by which mankind may benefit sufficiently from contact with these so-called Elders to justify the attendant risks, I have ordered that the expedition be reported lost and its personnel declared dead.*"

So, Gutierrez thought, *he wants his cake while thinking up a way to eat it, too.* The edict provoked a buzz of angry surprise. Sebastiano spoke a few words of gutter Spanish, echoed in English and other languages, including Russian. There was derisive shouting from outside the ship.

"*Quiet!*" The general's family and friends were part of a public about to be told he was dead. He felt pain and realized he'd set his jaw hard enough to break a tooth. Veins pulsed in his forehead and neck. He frowned at his cup, trying to breathe deeply and listen to the radio at the same time.

"... *on penalty of death, to send no further transmissions, which will be jammed in any event, nor to return to Earth. Do not acknowledge this transmission. Message ends.*"

Leaning awkwardly over Sebastiano's chair, Gutierrez bent the colonel's mike toward his own lips. At the same time, he stretched an arm behind him, letting the last few drops of coffee slip over the rim of his cup.

"Message received and understood," he told the Banker, disobeying the man's final order. As coffee splattered to the deck after its long fall in one-tenth gravity, he added, "Before signing off for good, I want you to hear this: I hereby rechristen this spacecraft *Laika!*"

III
Out on Elba

"You can't say that!"

Empleado pushed through the small crowd gathered around the general. The KGB agent's expression was frightened, but his face was red with fury. When he spoke, Gutierrez saw little gobbets of saliva burst from his lips.

"You're talking to the goddamned *Banker*! Don't you realize—"

"You're losing it, Art." Ortiz, who'd replaced Richardson as captain of the *Wright*, was the one man in the expedition shorter than its commander. Broad as he was short, scuttle-butt had it that his great-great-grandfather had been a Yaqui chieftain. The general straightened and turned toward him, but didn't interrupt. "What can Deshovich do to us that hasn't been done already, maroon us on an asteroid?"

"He could—" Empleado stopped, jaw hanging. People laughed at him, a sound he couldn't have heard much since beginning his career. He closed his mouth, realizing for the first time, perhaps, that the Banker's threats were empty: Earth's only spacegoing vessels were right here. And apparently it hadn't dawned on him before now that he was cut off from his source of power. Around him, more faces broke into appreciative grins. Even Pulaski was enjoying his discomfiture in her sheepish way. They couldn't get home, was the thought they all shared—all but the KGB man—but on the other hand, home couldn't get them, either.

For Gutierrez, among others, it meant a war was over before it started. The last time he'd been summoned to the radio this way, he'd been ordered by his now-"retired" leaders to use his forty-two-person "force," mostly scientific and technical personnel with little or no combat training, to drive the nautiloids off the asteroid. The fact that this would pit a handful of shotguns, rifles, and sidearms obsolete even on Earth against pocketable nuclear plasma weapons half a billion years more advanced hadn't counted with politicians who didn't have to live with the consequences.

One of those consequence was visible about him now, automatic pistols in flapped military holsters slapping the legs of engineers and laboratory types who'd never even handled a gun before. Better acquainted with such lethal hardware, Sebastiano not only carried a nonregulation Glock 9m/m instead of the official CZ99A1 chambered for the .41x22 cartridge the American military issued (his privilege as a command-level officer), but leaning against the console beside him was a 12-gauge semiautomatic Remington from which he'd become inseparable the past couple of days.

Even Gutierrez, to his astonishment, found himself lugging not one but two handguns, picked up when their owners had no further use for them. At the time he'd been less concerned with self-defense than with keeping dangerous toys out of careless hands. The stainless, short-barreled Smith & Wesson .44 magnum (even more nonregulation, if possible, than Juan's Glock) had been Kamanov's, smuggled like the cigarettes he knew his son Danny was responsible for. The Israeli SD9 was evidence that Richardson had been Russian KGB; they were known to favor the tiny pistol. Both guns dragged at his pockets. If it weren't for the one-piece garment he wore, they'd have long since pulled his pants down. Tired of the weight, he was somehow reluctant to give it up. It was the first time in his life, the aging fighter pilot thought with irony, that he'd relied on any weapon costing less than a hundred million dollars.

Behind him, he heard Eichra Oren clear his throat.

"Excuse me, General, I'm afraid I lack a referent. Would you mind explaining the significance of the name 'Laika'?"

Before Gutierrez could respond, there was another interruption. "Why is this man on the command deck," Empleado demanded, glaring at Eichra Oren, "armed with a dangerous weapon! He isn't a member of this expedition!"

Displacement activity. The behaviorist phrase welled up in the general's memory, heard at a leadership seminar he'd been required to attend years ago and remembered because of his fondness for cats. Empleado complained about an edged weapon when he was surrounded by guns, attacking Eichra Oren the same way a cat washes itself furiously when you catch it up to no good. Only now did Gutierrez consciously notice the sword hanging at Eichra Oren's thigh. It should have been the first thing anyone noticed about him. Somehow it never was.

"You know as well as I do, Art," he didn't try to hide his exasperation, "that Eichra Oren is serving as an observer for the Elders. That 'dangerous weapon' is his badge of office and he's never without it." He was tempted to ask what good a nondangerous weapon would be. "Try thinking of it as a naval officer's saber. It's the same kind of thing."

Empleado was unmollified. "Yes, General, but unlike the unsharpened butterknives affected by our Navy, this is more than a ceremonial accessory!"

The remark, Gutierrez knew, was meant for Ortiz, recently transferred to AeroSpace. But Empleado had him; the Elders had no concept of divided powers. Not only did Eichra Oren serve as policeman and judge, he was also an executioner, killing with his hands and a fusion-powered pistol as well as with the sword. Summoned as what he termed a 'p'Nan moral debt assessor' when it appeared that Semlohcolresh had murdered Kamanov, he'd completed his task quickly and with greater success than even he might have wished: the affair had ended with his collecting on the unpayable moral debt murder creates by taking the life of Reille y Sanchez, with whom, Gutierrez knew, he had by then fallen in love. The whole thing had been tragically stupid, but had served to delay a suicidal little war it now looked like they wouldn't have to fight. Whatever else he'd had to say, the Banker hadn't mentioned those earlier orders.

The Elders' envoy had been briefed on present-day Earth before arrival. Gutierrez had been impressed over the past few days with their sources of information, along with whatever technique the man had applied not only to learn facts, but English, Spanish, and Russian. It appeared, however, that there were gaps in his understanding of human history and culture.

"At the beginning of space exploration," Gutierrez turned to Eichra Oren, determined to ignore Empleado if he couldn't outargue him, "we'd been putting small things into orbit. America managed to send up rats or mice, recovered for later examination, or maybe that was just the plan. In any case, the Russians, not to be outdone, sent up a big payload with a little sled dog named Laika. All over the world, everybody thought that was quite a feat—until the Russians admitted they couldn't get her down again and had never intended to. She died slowly, of suffocation."

"I see," Eichra Oren frowned. Controlling his scabbard with one hand, he reached to give his dog a reassuring pat. "And this new leader—"

"*Self-appointed* leader!" Whoever had interrupted immediately withdrew into the crowd. Gutierrez suspected it was Danny.

"Self-appointed leader," Eichra Oren agreed. "As far as he knows—"

"*Or cares!*" Gutierrez didn't bother to look. Smuggler, seditionist, where in God's name had he and the boy's mother gone—on second thought, given recent experience, maybe they'd brought the kid up right, after all.

Eichra Oren was persistent. "As far as he knows or cares, he's stranded his own people here forever, until your consumables run out and you die just like that little dog, of suffocation, starvation, or the cold of space."

Gutierrez nodded. He knew that Eichra Oren had voluntarily marooned himself on this asteroid, at least for the time being, a necessity to which he'd been resigned from the beginning. Even so advanced a species as the Elders, with an evolutionary head start of five hundred million years and an equivalent technological lead, found travel between alternate universes difficult and dangerous. "Or left to whatever mercy a bunch of alien monsters—meaning the people you work for—offer us. Whether he knows that we won't suffocate or freeze—"

"Thanks to the way," Eichra Oren interrupted, raising his eyebrows toward the canopy a kilometer overhead which lent a greenish tint to everything beneath it, "the Elders have terraformed this place?"

"You still don't get the point," Gutierrez told the Antarctican. "I've only just seen it, myself. I'm not sure I knew myself why I held that little rechristening ceremony. Simple defiance, maybe. But look: it was a small thing, one poor little husky bitch. People get used to hearing of all kinds of evil happening to other people and they never seem to learn much from it. But animals—I've never been a great animal lover, Eichra Oren, but what happened with that little dog, the calculated coldbloodedness of it, should have told us all we needed to know about socialism."

"*General!*" Empleado gasped.

"The 'us' is figurative, of course"—Gutierrez was unrelenting—"it was long before my time. I always thought there should have been bonfires in the streets the next day, the works of Marx, all kinds of leftist magazines and books, set ablaze by those who wrote and edited and published them—and now had reason to know better. That should have been followed by the collapse of America's most successful homegrown socialists, the Democrats and Republicans. But there weren't, it wasn't, and it was the last clear warning we ever got."

"*General!*"

"Sorry, Art, there's nobody to tattle to any more." Gutierrez turned to Eichra Oren. "When I was a kid, a cartoon showed up in the underground papers called *Out On Elba*. It was set on an island only a couple of meters across and only had a couple of characters.''

Eichra Oren smiled. ''All there was room for, probably.''

''Probably.'' Gutierrez smiled back, mostly at the childhood memory. ''The main character was the 'Little Corporal,' pudgy, with a face that reminded you of a snail. You know, *escargot*? He was supposed to represent power put in its place, but you sort of felt sorry for him. His only companion was a pig with a crown who was supposed to be a reincarnated Louis XIV.''

''I get it,'' Sebastiano put in, ''King of the Franks!''

Gutierrez watched the colonel struggle from the embrace of the command chair. ''I hadn't thought of that, Juan. Louis the Pig was so fat his feet wouldn't touch the ground, and he wasn't very good company, always mumbling, '*L'Etat c'est moi*.' The Little Corporal would watch ships on the horizon and wish he were a seagull so he could escape. He once said: 'Exile, like the Academy Award, is an honor. It only *seems* unbearable because you can't share it with all the little people who made it possible.''

There was no outright laughter this time, but he got appreciative smiles, those of machinist Corporal Owen and life support officer Lieutenant Lee Marna among them. Sedition appeared to be contagious. Eichra Oren grinned at Empleado, addressing Gutierrez. ''Maybe there are exceptions.''

Empleado reddened again. ''General, I demand that you disarm this loudmouth immediately and eject him from the ship!''

Gutierrez laughed. ''You disarm him, Arthur, I'd like to see that!''

''General!'' Roger Betal, the former thug who now avoided his KGB boss, pushed in excitedly. Beside him was Staff Sergeant C. C. Jones, mission information officer (if all this was ever made public) and stringer for *American Truth*, a former anchorman retired when he'd suddenly begun speaking with a slur. Gutierrez had forgotten Jones over the past few days. He'd opposed his being in the expedition in the first place. Twenty years ago, with the USA in the last throes of becoming the ASSR, Gutierrez had commanded the famous Redhawk Squadron, suppressing guerrilla resistance. He and Jones had argued over some bright lights, as useful to enemy snipers as to a TV crew, during nighttime efforts to disarm a bomb placed in one of his interceptors where it sat on a runway apron. Gutierrez had won the argument by knocking out the lights—and Jones's teeth—with a fire extinguisher.

"... giant centipede," Betal was saying. Gutierrez decided he'd better pay attention. "It just walked into camp! Eichra Oren, it says it wants to talk to you!" The assessor was responsible for Betal's disaffection, having won the man's admiration by humiliating him in unarmed combat.

Eichra Oren raised a hand before Empleado could speak. "I was just going anyway. That's my friend Scutigera outside." To Gutierrez, Sebastiano, and Ortiz: "General, Colonel, Major. Coming, Sam?"

"Gladly." The dog bared its teeth at Empleado. "Some of the company around here stinks!"

IV
Insider Trading

Stooping out through the oval portside crewhatch at the middeck of the *Moynihan*, Eichra Oren clambered over the upturned edge of the plastic-coated wire-mesh basket in which the shuttle and its fleetmates had been lowered to the surface. As his feet touched the ground, he discovered that his friend Scutigera was the center of considerable—if ambivalent—attention.

Most of the humans huddled beneath the stubby wings of their spacecraft, all eyes turned toward Scutigera. Nor was it difficult for him to dominate the scene, even without moving a limb. Nine meters from his rounded, intelligent-looking head with its pair of huge, glittering compound eyes to the final segment of his tapered body, he took up even more space than that implied, since his graceful antennae and many of his fifteen pairs of slender legs were longer yet.

Eichra Oren had always thought Scutigera a handsome being. His legs and antennae were banded in contrasting shades of brown, his body patterned with what the newcomers would have termed "racing stripes." Beneath his head he bore three pairs of jaws, the rearmost vestigial (his remote ancestors had wielded poisoned fangs), the others specialized for manipulation. His people were the largest land sapients Eichra Oren knew of (and his knowledge was extensive), but they were subtle and accomplished technologists, producing, long before their first contact with the Elders, everything from nuclear steam turbines to watches with moving parts invisible to the naked human eye.

"Well, old crustacean." Sam spoke first, an attention getter in itself for the dazed humans clustered under the spacecraft. Some, in a setting that afforded one shock after another, hadn't yet heard about his artificially enhanced intelligence. "You still know how to make an entrance!"

Adroit for a creature of his size, Scutigera slewed his first few segments around and let his antenna-tips patter greetings along Sam's muzzle and then Eichra Oren's cheeks. Several beneath the shuttle wings groaned and turned away. From within the giant sapient came a low, cultivated voice, speaking the language of ancient, lost Antarctica. "Oasam, my furry and infuriating friend, as I have told you on many previous occasions, I am an arthropod, not a crustacean. How would you enjoy being called a reptile?"

"Some of my best friends," Sam replied in the trilling tongue of a world in which warm-blooded dinosaurs had survived global catastrophe to become Earth's sapient race, "are reptiles." If he sounded pleased with himself, it was because they were no more reptilian than Scutigera was crustacean.

"Hopeless," the centipede complained, still in the language of the Lost Continent. "Ah, well—my warmest greetings, Eichra Oren. Kindly inform me of the health and happiness of your esteemed mother, Eneri Relda. And why haven't you sent this beast to obedience school?"

"He wouldn't go." Eichra Oren grinned up at the inhuman face hovering above his own. "My mother is well, happy, and busy, as usual. This is a surprise, old friend, I wasn't even aware you were in this universe until I received your signal just now." He tapped the side of his head where, as with all sapients associated with the Elders, sophisticated electronics had been implanted on his cortex, similar to the device that raised Sam's intelligence from that of an unusually bright dog to that of a human being.

"I am a partner in the enterprise." Scutigera waved meters of antenna in a shrug. "How could I deprive myself of one of Mr. Thoggosh's adventures? They're inevitably diverting—at my age a greater consideration than you might imagine—and almost always indecently profitable. Speaking of our mutual molluscoid associate, he would appreciate your presence in his chambers at your earliest convenience. I came, supposing that you might prefer riding with me to risking life and limb in one of his flying bagels."

In fact he preferred the electrostatic aerocraft Scutigera mentioned, but visiting with his old comrade was a pleasant prospect. They'd shared many an adventure, but it was long since they'd seen each other. "American culture," he chuckled, "is getting to be a—what's the word, Sam, for an enthusiasm pursued en masse?"

"Fad." The dog rolled his eyes in appeal to Scutigera.

"Too lazy to access his own implant—and if it's all the same to you, I'll walk."

"There's a stop I want to make," the man declared, "about halfway between here and Mr. Thoggosh's residence."

Scutigera bent several legs, lowering his front quarters to assist as Eichra Oren clambered astride the first segment behind the arthropod's head. Smoothly polished, toast-colored chitin made a precarious perch. Resting his sword across his thighs, the man waved to his fellow humans as the arthropod's first stride, rippling through the ranks of his many legs like a kick through a chorus line, whisked them out of the camp and plunged them into the jungle surrounding it. Sam trotted along beside them, not quite forced to break into a lope. In addition to being the largest land sapients Eichra Oren knew of, Scutigera's people were among the swiftest, their present breathtaking pace representing no more than a stately crawl to the giant.

"I observe," Scutigera commented once they found themselves deep within the lush, dripping forest, "that you do not permit the prospect of a prolonged stay on this asteroid to disturb you. But then you are a multitalented being, well capable of filling any number of productive roles, and I could not help noticing the presence here of many attractive females of your species. . . ."

The joke was old between them. Scutigera's mating season was limited, requiring drastic physiological changes before it became even mechanically possible. Like all sapients he had an excellent memory, especially for pleasure. Despite his unusually high tolerance for differing customs, he envied those capable of recreational mating. It was a measure of his fundamentally good nature that, rather than resenting what he saw as an immutable fact of life, he teased his friends among more fortunate species about it.

A flock of pink, long-legged birds of a kind Eichra Oren had never seen before flew over, making an absurd racket. Gripping the weapon which was his honor and burden, he shook his head, knowing the gesture would be visible within his friend's 360 degrees of peripheral vision. The topic of females was a bit tender at the moment and might remain so for some time, so he pushed it out of his mind. If the ride atop the giant arthropod was slippery, it was smooth, taking place as it did on so many points of suspension. From the timbre of his voice, he might have been speaking from an armchair.

"Life serves its purpose simply by being lived," he replied, "and to me, it doesn't much matter where. As you probably know, Mr. Thoggosh required my services here as an assessor. . . ."

"One could hardly miss an event which generated such heated debate," the giant centipede replied. No Elder, nor any among the many species associated with them, could abide an unpaid moral debt, especially one owed by himself. It was customary to resolve personal and business disputes, and to examine one's own conscience periodically, with the aid of professional assessors wise in the half-billion-year-old philosophy of *p'Na* and capable of prescribing measures to restore the balance. This didn't often require literal use of the assessor's sword, but it was there if need arose. "I collected over a year's income in gold and platinum, wagering on your decision with unfortunates less well informed concerning your habits of mind. Although considering how it ended, perhaps I oughtn't to admit to such crassness."

Eichra Oren laughed. Whatever they'd accomplished on their own before discovery by the Elders, Scutigera's folk, like many primitive societies, had never reconciled what they imagined to be moral perfection—altruistic self-sacrifice—with personal material gain. This contradiction had resulted in the downfall of countless otherwise admirable civilizations and was taken seriously by the Elders as a symptom of potentially fatal disorder. Adopting *p'Nan* ethics had solved the problem at a conscious level for the centipede people, yet Eichra Oren knew that with cultures as well as individuals, it is the oldest, most self-destructive habits that die the most lingering death.

"Even the Americans have a proverb about an 'ill wind,'" he said. "Or was it 'insider trading'? In any case, the task is done, thanks to *p'Na*. I'm glad someone benefited by it. Now I've set out to accomplish what may prove far more difficult: understanding my fellow humans and the bizarre, twisted culture they've created."

Antennae waved in agreement. "They are a strange people, Eichra Oren."

"You said a mandible-full!" Sam volunteered, sounding out of breath. The man knew that he regretted not accepting a ride, although how he'd have stayed atop their friend's slippery carapace defied speculation.

"Stranger than you can possibly imagine," he told the arthropod. "You know that their *leaders*"—the alien concept had to be rendered in English—"somehow obliged the expedition's members, in such a manner that many of them felt they must comply even if it meant dying, to drive us off this asteroid by force, despite Mr. Thoggosh's unquestioned prior claim and our obviously overwhelming numerical and technical superiority."

"So I gather," Scutigera answered. "I was warned when they arrived that a collective willingness to countenance outright thievery and an individual capacity to ignore the facts of objective reality are indispensable civic virtues in American culture. Or perhaps it was religious virtues—it seemed so absurd at the time that I don't remember clearly now. How could such a people have survived the rigors of natural selection?"

"Civil *and* religious. They've acquired a reflexive aversion to plain, inconvenient truth, and they're ready to vote away anyone's life, liberty, or property, even their own, if that'll help them pretend it doesn't exist. In any case, through this mysterious power to impose ridiculous obligations, these *leaders* caused a murder, apparently intended as a provocation to general violence—although why they thought it would serve that purpose, I still don't understand; it makes no sense to blame a whole people for the act of a single individual. But now, as the Americans say, it's academic—"

"Telling us much," Sam offered, "about their educational systems."

"Since their *new* leader has abandoned them," Eichra Oren finished.

Scutigera chuckled. "I reiterate my question about natural selection."

"Now for the really confusing part," the man mused. "Horatio Gutierrez, another of these *leaders* although in some ways he reminds me of Mr. Thoggosh, seems almost relieved to be abandoned. More, I think, than can be accounted for by any last-minute cancellation of hostilities I don't believe he ever planned to commence. He even makes jokes about it. Comprehending that alone ought to fully occupy my time here. . . ."

Scutigera slowed the pace. "And?"

"There's no deceiving you, is there, old friend?" He shook his head. "All right, I find I'm not overly eager to go home. There remain some aspects of this recent assessment I must think through. For one, although I haven't any doubt that I executed my office correctly, I find I don't look forward to telling my mother about what happened. I'm uncertain why. So for the time being, I'm content—"

"Ask if *I'm* content!" interrupted Sam, tired of keeping up. "How many females of *my* species have you seen around this free-floating dungball?"

Again Scutigera chuckled. "It was always my impression, Otusam, that you prefer females of the human species."

"—and confident," the man ignored the byplay, "that we'll get home eventually, when and if the Elders stumble across whatever they're looking for here. By the way, old friend, you wouldn't happen to know what that is, would you?" Here, Eichra Oren thought, trying not to be seen holding his breath, was the most fascinating and annoying mystery of all. The challenge of solving it, despite his employer's determination to keep him in the dark, was a primary reason he didn't mind staying on 5023 Eris.

"You weren't informed?" The arthropod's tone was ironic. "It pains me to say that if I did know—and I don't say either way, *old friend*—I couldn't say. Conditions of strictest secrecy were agreed upon in the first clause of the contract I signed with Mr. Thoggosh."

Eichra Oren was silent. Proprietary secrets were certainly no novelty in the Elders' free-trade society. Nor was it impermissible, within bounds of *p'Na*, for others to ferret them out and make what use of them they might. Still, this was an enormous undertaking even for them to keep under wraps, involving (he hadn't needed the numbers before this; now they scrolled past his mind's eye via implant) thousands of beings on this one asteroid alone, plus how many more—that many?—in support roles back in the home universe.

How often had he heard Mr. Thoggosh say that two can keep a secret as long as one is dead and the other frozen in liquid nitrogen? Shrugging, he blinked away the display.

"Slow down, old friend, this is where I want to stop."

V
The Scene of the Crime

He'd dreaded this moment for what seemed like weeks.

In fact, it had only been a couple of days. Yet Eichra Oren knew that the exercise (which was how he thought of it), however difficult or painful it proved, was necessary to his peace of mind. A matter of tying up loose ends. Not long ago he'd remarked that life consists of little besides loose ends and that often they were the only thing that gave survivors a reason for going on. The way things had turned out, he had been speaking to someone who *hadn't* survived.

A great distance overhead, he spotted a tiny black dot against the yellow canopy, one of Scutigera's "flying bagels," coming from the direction of the human camp toward the Elders' settlement. Wondering idly who it was, he slid, sword in hand, from Scutigera's back, landing lightly on his feet (given his training and condition, he'd have landed lightly anyway) in the low gravity.

Neither noticing nor caring whether his friends followed—a heroic feat of shutting out the world considering that one of them was a talking dog and the other nine meters from antenna-tip to toe-claw—he pushed a curtain of leafy branches out of the way, each motion of his body stirring memories burned into his brain by later events, to cross a little creek he recognized, and began working his way upstream along its low bank. The air felt cool and moist, laden with the oddly mixed perfumes of fresh growth and decaying forest debris. For a few heartbeats, an iridescent blue-green dragonfly hovered over his shoulder like a singing jewel before darting off on some predatory errand. In the end, he came to a miniature waterfall that broke the stream's course at the sprawling foot of an enormous canopy tree.

Not more than forty-eight hours ago (although he realized all over again that it seemed much longer), he'd stood on this exact spot with a peculiar object in the palm of his hand, knowing it would resemble an undersized golf ball to the person he was showing it to, complete to color and texture.

"My office and personal quarters," he'd told her, "at least it will be in a few days. It's a seed with engineered genes. Be careful not to drop it or it'll try to take root." He'd stepped to the tree, reaching as high as he could, and touched the object to the trunk. When he'd taken his hand away, the seed had stayed in place. "When it matures," he remembered saying with a glibness that made him feel a bit ashamed now, "it'll cantilever out over the stream and I can fall asleep listening to the waterfall."

Drawing sustenance from the tree (equally engineered to tolerate the process), the new growth jutted out now like a shelf mushroom, still days away from the intended size and shape. All nautiloid construction on the asteroid had been accomplished this way, by living things designed at a molecular level to grow and die, leaving skeletons of titanium or plastic as coral leaves a skeleton of calcium, preconceived rather than prefabricated. On the way here with Sam and Scutigera, he'd persuaded himself that he wanted to check on the progress of the seed he'd planted. He was weary of his impersonal temporary quarters in the Elders' complex, wearier still of the forced companionship they necessitated, at meals for example. A need for solitude throbbed within him like a toothache. But at this particular moment he couldn't imagine dwelling on this spot. He had more compelling reasons for being here.

He and his guest had found a mossy place to sit at the base of the tree. Listening to the waterfall—in the clearer, deeper water a meter away, a handful of silver minnows darted and gleamed—he'd explained that the site he'd chosen was exactly halfway between the human and the nautiloid camps. This seemed appropriate, since it more or less described his own position. Had circumstances been different he'd have gone on to say that, as a human brought up with the outlook and values of the Elders, he'd felt a bit lost since coming to 5023 Eris and at the same time caught in the middle. Had circumstances been different, he'd have asked her . . .

Instead, he'd accused her of a series of terrible crimes, tricked her into confessing, dealt with her in the customary manner of a moral debt assessor, assisting her to pay the token (it could be no more than that) for three lives she'd taken with far less concern than he was showing her. And now the thought of living and working here—but that was pointless. Suppose somebody lived as long as Mr. Thoggosh— or his own mother—indulging in the kind of fetishism that made him avoid every place where something painful had occurred: eventually there wouldn't be anyplace he could go, anything he could do, that wouldn't carry with it some unbearable association.

"So the criminal does return to the scene of the crime!"

He turned, startled not so much by the presence of another person as by the fact that he hadn't noticed her until now. The first thing that impressed him about Rosalind Nguyen, here in the deep, kilometer-tall forest, was how tiny she looked. She wasn't the least bit frail; at the moment she seemed the most solid thing present. Her eyes were huge and dark, her skin the color of antique gold. Only as an afterthought did he open his mouth to protest the injustice of her words. Stepping toward him around the canopy tree, hands in her trouser pockets, she cut him off simply by raising her eyebrows.

"Forgive me, Eichra Oren, that was unkind and untrue. I just—well, it was there inside me to say." She scuffed at loose leaves lying on the ground and smiled, her eyes crinkling at the corners in a way that appealed to him. If his culture had used the same conventional symbolism as hers, he'd have described her face as heart-shaped, its lines beginning with a small, almost pointed chin, sweeping upward through pleasing curves and angled cheekbones to a broad, intelligent brow. Her hair was black as space, unusually fine in texture. "Now that it's said, at least I don't have to think it anymore."

They'd spoken several times in camp, but never like this, out of sight of the others. He was unaware that, like many Oriental English speakers of even the third or fourth generation, she spoke with something that wasn't quite an accent, a lingering habit of family speech or even some minor difference of structure nobody but a physical anthropologist would know or care about. What he heard he might have called a lilt. Sensitive as he was to language and the sound of words, he only knew that he enjoyed listening to her.

"What are you doing here?" He cleared his throat. The question hadn't come out as he'd intended, but like his idea of a police interrogation.

She shrugged, unoffended, a pretty gesture he surprised himself by hoping was uncalculated. "Trying to figure out what happened here—not the facts, I know them all too well—just how I feel about them, what they mean. Yours is a strange culture, Eichra Oren. It prefers its charity and brutality in unmixed portions."

The statement was so full of false assumptions that he didn't know where to begin setting her straight. She'd have done the necropsy, of course, and that would be influencing her. She was standing beside him now, looking up into his eyes, close enough that he caught the clean scent of her hair. That and the way she'd said his name suddenly made it difficult to think. Reille y Sanchez had had the same effect on him. What was it about these American women?

"I—"

He wanted to argue, tell her that whatever favors the Elders had done for her people, they hardly constituted charity. More important, the act of judgment, of justice, he had committed in this place had been the opposite of brutality. Somehow the words wouldn't come and he dragged himself to a halt at the first stupid-sounding syllable, unwilling to compound inanity.

Again she smiled. "Don't misunderstand me, Eichra Oren, that's not a criticism." She lifted a small, slender hand as if to lay it on his forearm, then let it drop. He saw, with the involuntary eye of a reflexive observer, that it had that look of transparent parchment—not as unattractive as it sounded—which came from a physician's practice of washing dozens of times a day. "At least I don't believe it is. . . ."

He'd noticed before that Americans had characteristic reflexes of their own. At the moment, she was looking around to make sure they weren't being overheard, unaware she was doing it. He encouraged her with a nod.

She got it out in a rush: "It might even result in a happier world."

That was the very point he'd come here to ponder, although he found, somewhat to his chagrin, that he was less interested in what she was saying than in how she looked as she said it, the way she moved, the way her mouth, her lips, her tongue, her small white teeth had with the words they made.

"That's interesting. Tell me why you think so."

She was still tentative. "You have to understand that everything about life the way we humans lead it—"

"You humans?" He suppressed an impulse to step back. What was implied by that phrase, even unintentionally, disappointed him. But at least, as she struggled to deal with her own awkwardness, he caught his breath, getting his conversational bearings again.

"I mean . . ." She looked down at her small feet, keeping her eyes on the mossy ground, obviously feeling as self-conscious as he did. It was easier for her to speak to him this way, focused on battered kevlar and neoprene rather than his face. ". . . those of us from Soviet America, from the United World Soviet, from our version of Earth. Everything about life there has always felt, to me, sort of murky and diluted at the same time—"

He bent, tilting his head to look up into her eyes, resisting an urge to reach out and lift her chin. Aside from the effect her small, well-shaped breasts and slender waist—contours easily discernible under her soft, well-worn shipsuit—seemed to be having on his endocrine and circulatory systems (how could this be happening so soon after what he'd just gone through with Estrellita?), she was the first of these people who promised to make anything resembling sense. He didn't want to spoil it.

"What do you mean, 'everything,' Dr. Nguyen?"

"Nobody here but us Rosalinds." She looked up at him.

"I seem to have left my doctorate, and any wisdom I ever managed to acquire with it, back in camp. Or back on Earth, maybe. I don't know what I mean, Eichra Oren, the moral atmosphere, I suppose."

She shrugged, this time with tension and frustration, folded her hands, and pressed the heels of her palms together. The tips of her left fingers were callused. He remembered seeing a stringed instrument in camp and guessed— in his profession guesses were as important as deductions— that she seldom played for others. It wouldn't suit her character. Whatever music she made would serve her as a means of relaxation, meditation, even therapy.

"Polluted," she went on, "and at the same time lacking enough oxygen. At home all of our favorite homilies condemn seeing things in black and white. But that's the way I see them, Eichra Oren, the way I always have. I must, doing what I do, or people who are counting on me die. That's why I think I understand what happened here. There's a cleanliness in the way your people address moral issues, as if they were engineering problems, a genuine aspect of reality, that I find—whatever it reveals about me—exhilarating, like a mountain breeze blowing away the cloying humidity of a swamp."

He grinned at her. "Or the miasma of Marxism?"

"Nobody believes in that superstitious rot any more," she protested. "But somehow it seems to lead a life of its own no matter what anybody believes. And whenever anything important has to be done, we spend half of our precious time and energy giving it lip service, frightened to death that the other guy will turn out to be orthodox and expect it of us."

He searched his recently acquired memories. "Comrade Grundy?"

She smiled. "She's probably trapped like the rest of us. The awful part is that you can never tell, nobody wears a sign, and the price for guessing wrong is terrible. Even once that's settled, we waste the other half of our time and energy trying to find ways around constraints imposed by the belief system itself. You should see the contortions our geneticists go through just because Saint Karl backed the wrong theory of evolution!''

''Not to mention your economists. You're saying that, with the exception of occasional dangerous believers, you're compelled to live with Marxism the way your Western civilization was compelled to live, however uncomfortably, with Christianity for... twenty centuries, wasn't it?''

She gave him a reevaluating look. ''That was before my time, Eichra Oren. As the saying goes, I'm an atheist, thank God. And 'our' Western civilization aside''—her eyes twinkled—''my ancestors were all Buddhists.''

Whatever he'd intended to say never got said. They turned at the sound of someone, something, crashing toward them through the dense underbrush. When he saw who it was, Eichra Oren realized that the racket had been a deliberate, polite warning.

It worried him when Sam was polite.

''Hiya, Doc. I hate to break this up, Boss, but the reluctant crustacean says he has klicks to go and promises to keep. And His Majesty Thoggosh the First is paging us again. Anyway, you two don't have as much privacy as you think. Rubber Chicken Alvarez has been watching from the bushes.''

''Garbage grinder, practical joker, and Peeping Tom.'' Rosalind shook her head. ''Somehow it doesn't surprise me at all.''

VI
Water Music

Gazing through the liquid medium he breathed at the pale, soft-bodied creature before him, Mr. Thoggosh shuddered. The varied, adventurous life he led threw him into contact with sapients of many species, yet sometimes even he felt overwhelmed by the unlovely appearance of his intimate associates.

This was among the worst. He was unaware that the revulsion he felt was akin to that experienced by mammalian sapience at having turned over a rock to see what squirms beneath it. Where, he thought, were this thing's graceful, powerful manipulators, its firm shell of striped and colorful calcium? The stubbed limbs were obscenely jointed, terminating in a clutch of grotesque wigglers that reminded him of the linings of intestines. Instead of a pair of large, thoughtful, bronze-colored eyes, slit pupiled, with reflective retinae, two hard little buttons glittered at him from a death white mallet of a face. Nothing about them, nor of the alien countenance they were set in, conveyed any hint of the intelligence he knew—although at present he had difficulty *feeling* that he knew it—resided behind them.

His moment of revulsion ebbed as it had a million times before. Again he merely saw humanity sitting before him, no more inherently evil, stupid, or disgusting than any sapience, every bit as capable of decency, brilliance, and nobility. He reminded himself that it was kin, through 750 generations, to his dear friend Eneri Relda and that fearsome hatchling of hers.

It was the first chance he'd had to interview this particular specimen, although he'd wanted to the moment he'd first heard of her. Until now, there simply hadn't been time. Complications seemed to arise of their own accord, one after another, in this enterprise he was attempting to direct on what some called 5023 Eris. Adding to his burdens was the difficulty of achieving a reasonable balance between kindness and justice in his relations with these beings who'd shown up on his property without having been invited. Someone, perhaps his assistant Aelbraugh Pritsch, had informed him that Eris was an ancient human deity associated with confusion. That seemed appropriate. He'd immediately adopted the name for an asteroid which heretofore had only been known by a serial designation.

"I'm a trifle curious about one thing," he continued a conversation that had been going on for several minutes without getting beyond the pleasantries both species were accustomed to, "if you don't mind my asking . . ."

This small, frail-looking female was considered timid even by her own cosapients. He realized he must be a rather imposing sight, resembling as he did "a giant squid with eyes the size of banjos." He must remember to ask Aelbraugh Pritsch what that meant; it was excerpted from one of the reports Gutierrez had sent Earthward. Add to that his sinuous, luminescent tentacles, not to mention an exoskeleton as large as a small personal vehicle of the previous century which his language software rendered "peoplecart," still beloved by the humans for some reason. He was gratified (and surprised) that he didn't seem to frighten her.

"Not at all, sir." Perched on the edge of a wire-mesh chair, Pulaski absently snagged a strand of floating hair and tucked it into place. Her earlier misgivings, he thought, over breathing the oxygenated fluorocarbon filling his quarters (for the benefit of nonaquatic visitors, he remembered with a trace of annoyance), seemed to be subsiding. "The more we all know about each other, the better."

Under a low ceiling, the walls of the long, wide room were obscure in the lighting he naturally favored, having evolved from abyssal organisms. Kelp plantings gave the place a homey feel and he'd brought here several favorite tactiles from his sculpture collection. Even to his own discriminating eye they appeared abstract, yet each was completely representational, playing on differences between touch and vision—in a manner analogous to human art based on optical illusion—to produce the kind of object he most enjoyed, that which appeared formless until physically engaged.

He laid one long tentacle over another. "I agree. And it occurs to me, Sergeant Pulaski, that our respective species have somewhat more in common than might first be expected. After all, I'm obviously a marine creature. And your species, of course, has a unique aquatic heritage all its own."

"Unique?" She sat up straight. "But Mr. Thoggosh, all life on Earth—on our Earth, anyway—began in the sea."

"I refer, my dear sergeant, to the millions of years your evolutionary predecessors spent paddling about the lakes and streams of Africa—having been driven from the trees by bigger, stronger monkeys—before they became formidable hunters of the veldt."

Pulaski sat back with an expression of disappointment. "Elaine Morgan, *The Descent of Woman*. It's just an old theory, Mr. Thoggosh, not very—"

"Ah, but look at yourself." He upturned another tentacle. "A mammal without fur except where it protects the head and shoulders from sunlight and water-reflected glare? A land animal with the subcutaneous fat reserves and respiratory reflexes of a cetacean? A female whose breasts—my dear, how can you stand naked before a mirror and doubt it?"

Pulaski blushed furiously. "I've never stood naked before a mirror."

"What a shame," the giant mollusc lied gallantly. "Yet any appreciation for beauty in others must begin with—"

"Mr. Thoggosh, don't con me." She folded her hands. He saw her knuckles whiten, understanding what it implied. "I wonder what you really know about us, whether you can even tell individual humans apart. I'm not sure I can tell individual nautiloids apart. Don't we all look alike to you?"

Having dealt with members of her species long before Pulaski's ancestors had rediscovered bronze, he found he learned more about them by listening than talking. His experience told him that something—he wasn't certain what, perhaps his very nonhumanity which made him, in her eyes, a nonjudgmental neutral—was about to plunge her into a self-revealing mood. He wasn't about to interfere with it; there was still too much to learn. Even had he been inclined to answer, he didn't get a chance as she rushed on.

"Well, we don't look alike to each other, and whatever anybody tells you, Mr. Thoggosh, looks count. When I was younger I remember hearing Somebody-or-other's Law to the effect that no woman is ever satisfied with the size of her breasts. Those with little ones want big ones and those with big ones complain of the inconvenience. Those in the middle—I don't know why I'm talking about this, but let me tell you, I would have been happy just to have more than what my dorm mates used to call 'fried hummingbird eggs.'"

"As you put it yourself, Toya, the more we know about each other..." He laid a gentle tentacle atop her hands, which appeared to be crushing one another, gratified that she didn't flinch from his cold molluscoid touch. "You're sure you don't care for something to drink? I'm having beer." As he withdrew (trying not to feel too relieved about it, himself), she shook her head, causing more of her fine brown hair to float free.

"No, thank you, Mr. Thoggosh."

To the left, his prized and beautiful songfish warbled sweetly in a cage suspended between floor and ceiling. He considered throwing something at it, wondering why he suddenly felt so irritable. True, Pulaski was the subject of his next talk with Eichra Oren, but no one had forced him to ask Scutigera to delay the debt assessor so that he might have her flown here for a preliminary interview. Perhaps this was the source of his annoyance. He regarded himself as an essentially simple being (which would have amused anyone who knew him) who pursued his goals straightforwardly. He sent his separable tentacle for beer, knowing as Pulaski watched the specialized limb detach itself from his body that it wouldn't be the shock to her it had been to the first American, General Gutierrez, who'd witnessed it. As it swam to the wall-cooler where he kept his kelp beer and returned with a container trailing a long sipping tube, he pushed the conversation onto a course he'd planned earlier.

"Toya, I've studied several hundred of the entertainments you call motion pictures. They have an equivalent among my people and tell a stranger much about the culture which created them." He sipped his beer, enjoying it as he always did. "Hence the trifling curiosity I mentioned earlier. With but rare exception, I've noticed that those among you with their reproductive anatomy hanging unprotected between their locomotory extremities—"

Her face reddened. "You mean men?"

"—nonetheless prefer garments consisting of two fabric cylinders which don't allow for that anatomy. Not one cylinder, mind you, not even three, which would make sense. Those among you without this anatomical liability, who might tolerate such attire, customarily wear only one cylinder."

Pulaski almost giggled, whether from tension or amusement he couldn't tell. She inhaled deeply, just as if she were breathing air. "There are Scotsmen, Mr. Thoggosh. And women have been wearing trousers quite a while, now." She brushed a hand down her patched and faded jumpsuit.

"Contrary to an irrationalism in which humans persist, exceptions neither prove the rule nor explain it." He took a sip of beer. Although his organs of speech and ingestion were independent, he'd acquired this useful habit of pacing conversation from his air-breathing associates and often wished he could smoke a pipe. "Similarly irrational, and vastly more hazardous, is this preference of your male gender for a wheeled transportation rack—"

"Give me a second." She frowned, then smiled, "You mean bicycles?"

"—with a horizontal structural member in just the position to inflict damage to the most vulnerable part of their bodies." He shuddered, imagining it. "Analogous female conveyances feature no such hazard."

Several heartbeats passed, his slow and ponderous, hers sounding to his acute hearing like the clatter of a small combustion engine. "I think it has less to do with . . . well, comparative anatomy than with the way men and women are expected to behave." She took a breath. "Traditionally, men are more active and aggressive. A man's bike needs that horizontal . . . member because harder use will be made of it. At the same time, a woman's bike has to accommodate the difference in clothing you spoke of."

"Rather than a difference in anatomy." He saw that his guess was correct: she was more at ease in his presence than among her cosapients. Curious about what caused such an attitude, he couldn't help wondering what advantage might be made of it. He lifted a tentacle in encouragement. "Kindly elaborate."

"As far as clothing's concerned, one cylinder might provide for the . . . difference. But it would catch on things and get in the way. Imagine a cowboy or a steelworker in a skirt." She giggled again. "And it's confining. Would you like a cloth cylinder wrapped around your—" She stammered to a stop, clearly realizing for the first time that he was naked.

" 'Tentacles' is acceptable, Toya." He set a dozen wiggling before her face. "I'm no more embarrassed by it than you by mention of your fingers."

She swallowed. "I never visited before with anyone who had tentacles."

"I see," he replied with a tolerant chuckle, then let his voice assume a more serious tone. "You fail to mention the emotional discomfort your species experiences with regard to its reproductive function. To a degree, one-cylinder garments conceal it. Two-cylinder garments disregard it altogether. But an active male wearing one cylinder would be in constant danger of humiliating exposure."

She closed her eyes and grimaced. "I'm just about the worst person you could ask about that, Mr. Thoggosh. In the first place, my primary interest is paleontology, not social anthropology, and in the second . . ."

"In the second," he observed, "discussing physical differences between the male and the female of your species embarrasses you."

"It does," she almost whispered. "It's just the way I am."

"It's the way you were brought up, my dear, to deny that aspect of your life which offers greatest satisfaction." He took a long draw on his beer, weighing his next words. "It's the same in many a primitive culture. Control *that* in a person through repression and guilt, and what you call 'society'—religion or the State—needn't control anything else about you in order to control you altogether, to bend you from healthy, natural inclinations toward its own, which are invariably less natural and considerably less healthy."

"People need direction," she protested. "You can't have them chasing any old selfish whimsy, living empty, meaningless lives. Isn't it better to serve some higher purpose, larger than yourself, than no purpose at all?"

"The concept of purpose," he replied, "is just that, Toya, an idea, a product of individual sapience. It didn't exist before sapience evolved. It's meaningless applied to a random, inanimate universe. Similarly, it's irrelevant—life having arisen from that randomness—to nonsapient organisms governed by simple tropisms and instincts generated in the trial-and-error process of mutation and natural selection."

"But—"

"If you seek purpose, use your own sapience, look within

yourself. Your life has one purpose only, to be lived as you wish. Beware anyone who claims otherwise: the mystic, the altruist, the collectivist. One life isn't enough for him—he wants to live his own and yours as well. His pleading and demands are baseless assertions thrown in the face of billions of years of evolution—itself without purpose, yet in response to natural law, invariably and unavoidably culminating in greater capacity, greater complexity, greater individuation—the very pinnacle of which, its crowning achievement and ultimate triumph over entropy, is self-directed intelligence.

"But this is small talk; I'd a practical reason for asking you here."

She appeared relieved and at the same time wary. "What's that?"

"Among other things, to benefit from the human, the Soviet American, point of view on a number of difficult questions which presently confront me." He lifted a tentacle in a negligent shrug. "For example, I'd like very much to know whether my guesses about your general's thinking are correct."

Now she frowned: "Why don't you ask him?"

"Because he's a busy sapient at the best of times and right now he has a headache on his hands. (Can you say that? Remarkable language.) I must know what his people are thinking, how well they see his reasons for doing things. I demand no betrayal, Toya, you needn't answer unless you wish to. But just now, General Gutierrez is thinking about the future, isn't he?"

"I suppose," she nodded, beginning to be interested, "we all are."

"And foremost among his thoughts must be this." He took a last sip and set the container aside, resisting the temptation to send for another. "If the United World Soviet has truly abandoned you, what's to become of thirty-odd surviving Soviet Americans on 5023 Eris?

"After all, you're completely dependent on alien monsters."

VII
Under the Microscope

"Alien monsters," Mr. Thoggosh repeated, his tone gentler now. "You needn't be self-conscious about thinking it, my dear, nor deny that you do. With the best intentions, I fear I often think it of people like yourself. However, in your case, they're monsters whose present kindness—"

She interrupted with a headshake. "What bothers me, sir, is that your 'present kindness' contradicts this 'Forge of Adversity' philosophy of yours, as we understand it."

"It's scarcely an impenetrable notion," he answered thoughtfully, "nor some arbitrary superstition you must accept as you might some primitive tribal custom of diet or attire. For millions of years we've understood, based on scientific reasoning open to reexamination at any time, that, as the product of eons of brutal weeding and pruning by natural selection, all sapients are the children of suffering and struggle."

"That's certainly grim." She gave him a brief, humorless smile.

"Not necessarily, Toya. After all, we've survived the process, something I think we're entitled to celebrate. And since successful struggle is what enabled us to become more than we were, hardier and brighter, we realize that shielding an individual or a species from what your poet termed 'the slings and arrows of outrageous fortune'—from being shaped and hardened in what we ourselves somewhat lyrically refer to as the 'Forge of Adversity'—however kindly the intention, represents the ultimate cruelty, depriving them, as it does, of their only motive or opportunity to transcend themselves.''

'' 'That which doesn't kill us makes us strong.' '' Pulaski pursed her lips in disapproval. ''Nietzsche, social Darwinism, dog eat dog, kill or be killed. Some humans have thought well of that philosophy. The Nazis, for example.''

''Do you blame Nietzsche or Darwin for being willfully misinterpreted to serve political ends?'' Mr. Thoggosh gave the equivalent of a resigned nod. ''But I see that like the Nazis, you'll read into my words what you will. That being the case, from your viewpoint, how long can our contradictory kindness be counted on? What will happen if it eventually runs out?''

'' *That* is the question.' '' She folded her hands in her lap, embarrassed. ''Sorry, you're the one who started quoting Hamlet.''

''Still, we approach the topic I wished to explore, nothing more than your general is asking himself this very moment: succinctly, in the otherwise hospitable environment of our terraformed asteroid, will you ultimately be allowed to starve to death where you sit? Might you find yourselves evicted altogether, to suffocate or freeze in the depths of space?''

Pulaski shivered. ''I wonder about that, myself.''

''I'm sure you do.'' Mr. Thoggosh paused to listen to a message coming over his implant. ''Another matter: what of his authority, if the government it derives from has truly disowned you? It's a measure of his character, as I understand it, that this won't occur to him until he's considered the more urgent subject of his people's survival—Toya, please excuse my momentary inattention. I've received word that Eichra Oren has arrived and will presently be joining us. That is, if you don't mind.''

''Why no,'' Pulaski answered, blinking. ''Why should I?''

''Indeed.'' He noticed her countenance reddening again. Was this merely a demonstration of mammalian volatility or had he missed a nuance? Was his task about to prove easier than he'd believed? He had a deep distrust for things that came to him too easily. "To continue: authority is the lifeblood of your civilization, and this raises a number of questions. For example, is it exigent, in the absence of Earth-supported authority, that your expedition reorganize itself? If so, how is that to be accomplished?"

With a perplexed expression, she opened her mouth to reply.

"*In America,*" a familiar human voice offered as, instead of speaking, Pulaski turned in her chair to see Eichra Oren and Sam swimming toward them through the fluorocarbon haze, "the law requires everyone to vote or suffer fine and imprisonment. And the franchise, as they call it, was a powerful custom long before it became compulsory." The man backpaddled, settling to the floor. "Despite that fact— or because of it—they haven't had a truly free election since the nineteenth century."

Mr. Thoggosh chuckled. "A cynic might amend that to the eighteenth century, citing the view of William Marcy Tweed, infamous boss of Tammany Hall and New York's Democratic party, that he didn't give a damn who did the voting as long as he did the nominating. Good morning, Eichra Oren, Otusam, it's gratifying to see you at last. May I offer you something? I'm having beer."

"Coffee, thanks." Eichra Oren waited as a chair descended from the ceiling then strapped himself in to avoid floating. The tentacle brought him a container. Unlike the beer, it was surrounded by mirage from the heat of its contents. Sam wasn't equipped to deal with a sipping tube. He sat beside Eichra Oren's chair, wedging his hindquarters under one leg in lieu of seatbelt.

"They say," the dog remarked, "and on Toya's Earth, mind you, that if voting could change things, it'd be illegal."

"Doubtless." Mr. Thoggosh sipped his own drink. "The question remains, will the Americans hold an election to reconfirm the general's authority or choose a new leader? Will they consider it conducive to their survival?"

Eichra Oren grinned and glanced at Pulaski. "When has it ever been conducive to anyone's survival?"

Sam looked up. "I was going to say that."

"I'll have some coffee now, if it isn't any trouble." Pulaski overcame her shyness. "I also want to say that if you've heard of Boss Tweed—I remember the name dimly from school, mostly because of Thomas Nast, the cartoonist who introduced the elephant and donkey—"

"As well as the Tammany Tiger." Her host sent his tentacle to the wall again. "Sugar? Milk? Cinnamon? Chocolate? Brandy? You'd be surprised at the things various sapients put in their coffee."

"But not that they all drink it?" She shrugged. "I guess I'll try milk and chocolate—thanks—but that proves my point, doesn't it? The Tammany Tiger, I mean. You've been studying more than old movies."

Mr. Thoggosh returned to his beer. "I'm sure you realize that your radio and television broadcasts—have I mentioned that your culture is uniquely noisy in that respect?—have been received, translated, and sifted by our computers for whatever information they may yield about you."

Pulaski took a dubious sip. "This is good! I know you've broken all our codes and—"

He made a many-tentacled gesture of denial. "Not 'broken,' Toya; they're simply susceptible to the same programming which sorts out all those thousands of signals from one another, eliminates natural and mechanical interference, and enhances signal-to-noise ratios."

She looked up from her drink. "Don't we have any right to privacy?"

"You maintain that what you fling into the air for anyone to receive is private? You're aware that we nautiloids have no voices in the sense you know. We communicate by natural, organic radio signals. At this moment, my words are being received, converted to sound, and relayed to you by those speakers against the walls. Must we stop our figurative ears—are we morally obliged to—because someone insists on shouting?''

Eichra Oren turned. ''And who do you mean 'we,' your government? Only individuals have rights, Sergeant. Proving that is a preschool exercise in our world. On the other hand, as far as I can see, your government recognizes no individual rights of any kind, let alone one to privacy.''

''Indeed,'' Mr. Thoggosh agreed, ''given the predilections of government, any eavesdropping we do seems like turnabout to me, and fair play.''

She lifted a defiant chin. ''It doesn't matter. I can't stop you.''

''No,'' the nautiloid agreed, ''you can't. What you, your general, or this Banker fellow have no way of realizing is that we know you even better than that. We have observed you with the minutest care since our initial unbeinged surveys of this asteroid, long before it was terraformed. We never interfered, although I confess the temptation's been all but overwhelming at times.''

She looked up again. ''You're talking over my head, Mr. Thoggosh.''

''And if I told you that we returned to this universe for the first time in fifteen thousand years in the late nineteenth century as you reckon it, the 1880s?''

''Observations,'' Eichra Oren added, ''peaked in the late 1940s.''

''About the time,'' Sam lifted a hind foot to scratch contemplatively at one ear, ''you people started dropping dirty little nukes on each other?''

Her eyes widened in honest surprise before self-conscious disbelief swept across her face to erase it. ''Flying saucers.''

''Interdimensional peepholes,'' her host replied. ''The objective ends, if you will, of survey devices based physically in our universe, rooted in the same technology which brought us to this place. They're handled rather like the beam of a flashlight. As you know, the use of such energies entails side effects—secondary discharges, conspicuous coronal displays—hence an occasional awareness of it by your people, despite the fact that our devices never created apertures larger than—''

''Like a flashlight beam,'' she repeated. ''No wonder they could do right angles at six-thousand klicks an hour! I guess there always was a certain small percentage of UFO sightings never properly accounted for.''

The mollusc regarded her. ''And a greater percentage misaccounted for by nation-states reluctant to admit that they can't control every event within their borders. Yet all we ever did was watch—it's all we were capable of at the time—although the number of alleged landings and personal contacts we inspired among the more fanciful was instructive.''

She nodded, '' 'Intelligences vast and cold and unsympathetic'?''

''By turns, as seems required of us. I believe the proper quotation is 'intellects.' We can, of course, be quite as petty and irritable and sanguine as any species. However, unlike those Martians of Messrs. Wells and Welles, we've an Earth of our own and needn't regard yours or anybody else's with envious eyes. Also, we've managed to cure the common cold.''

She laughed. ''So what did all this . . . watching teach you about us?''

Mr. Thoggosh considered. ''In the main, that the less reliably an idea works, the more tenaciously you cling to it. Welfare payments drain your moral and economic vitality, so you approve more welfare. Criminal laws create crime where none existed previously, so you pass more laws. You defend yourselves from a tyranny you fear some foreign power may impose by imposing it on yourselves, then wonder why your freedom has evaporated. You brought the Nazis into this, so you've no one to blame but yourself: Hitler's rise to preeminence took place in a manner fully reflecting the will of a legal majority; the ruination of your own country was achieved on precisely the same basis. Had half a billion years' experience not prepared us to distrust majoritarianism, that surely would have done it.''

"People get the kind of government they deserve," Sam grinned, "whether they deserve it or not."

It was Pulaski's turn: "One of our philosophers, Will Rogers, or maybe Winston Churchill, said democracy's a terrible system but it's better than anything else that's ever been tried."

"The Boss Tweeds of your world," Mr. Thoggosh countered, "are careful never to let the Will Rogerses or Winston Churchills try a genuine alternative to majoritarianism. They do exist, Toya, and they don't necessarily involve dictators or kings. Who says—what objective evidence supports the notion—that the majority has ever been right about anything, anyway?"

"More to the point," Eichra Oren put in, "what gives a majority its power to compel? Unless we're talking about brute force, why should anyone have to go along just because one over half of their fellow beings demand it?"

Pulaski blinked. "Because it's better than fighting?"

Eichra Oren grimaced. "It *is* fighting, with none of the satisfactions."

"Well, how about strength in numbers, or 'Two heads are better than one,' or 'United we stand, divided we—'''

The nautiloid lifted a tentacle. "Toya, such attributes as virtue or intelligence aren't additive. It's absurd to maintain that two evil people can somehow be more virtuous than one decent person or that two stupid people are brighter than one intelligent person. Why, then, does your culture assume that two people possess more rights than one?"

"I wish I could give you an answer." She peered about with that reflex Eichra Oren had mentioned, as if she feared being overhead. "We're not encouraged to think about things like that."

"Whose interest does that serve?" Mr. Thoggosh waved the rhetorical question away. "Never mind, Toya, skipping theory and fastening upon the urgently pragmatic, what if by some horrible—but typical—miscarriage of democracy, Arthur Empleado, let us say, were chosen to lead your expedition?''

"I—''

"Alternatively, what would happen if you tried, individually or as a group, to join what you know as the Elders' culture? Other species have, and other individuals. Set aside the question of whether we would permit it. Certainly it won't be permitted by your superiors here. And are your leaders at home really out of it? This 'Banker' seems to have left contingencies open. If he should recontact you, which—unauthorized elections or alliance with us—will he consider more treasonous?''

"I don't know, Mr. Thoggosh, you're raising points I hadn't begun—''

"It might be well if you did, Sergeant. Difficult decisions will soon be required of you and your friends.'' This was the principal point Mr. Thoggosh had been working up to. He hesitated, knowing that if he succeeded now, it might save trouble for everyone in the near future. "It had occurred to me, given your interest and expertise in paleontology, a subject of importance to me at present, that I might hire you away from General Gutierrez. You'll regard my terms as unprecedentedly generous. What would your general say, and do you care one way or another? What would you say, Toya?''

She blinked with surprise. "I think I ought to pretend I didn't hear it—or any of the rest of this. I'm grateful, Mr. Thoggosh, believe me. I wish I could accept. But if Mr. Empleado were to find out—''

Pulaski shivered.

VIII
A Policeman's Lot

"*Laika*," Mr. Thoggosh chuckled. "Surely Mr. Empleado offered some comment on the general's attitude."

"Through clenched teeth, at the top of his lungs," Eichra Oren grinned. "I imagine it must have hurt." He willed himself off the chair-edge, trying to relax. Outside it would be afternoon by now. Pulaski had gone, presumably to ponder Mr. Thoggosh's offer although she'd made a pretense of turning it down. Sam, too, had run off on some errand. Furry sapients weren't happy soaking in liquid fluorocarbon, however temperate and oxygenated. Eichra Oren looked forward to leaving as well, having had enough of the aqueous gloom the great mollusc regarded as cozy, but which he often found depressing. "I'm ashamed to admit I enjoyed watching it," he told his employer. "It's slim return on the investment you're making keeping me around."

As they spoke, Mr. Thoggosh stabbed button after lighted button in the space before him set aside as a desk. In all fairness the atmosphere—or at least the tempo—had changed with the amateur paleontologist's departure. She'd been a guest; Eichra Oren was family. A backlog of urgencies had accumulated during each minute spent entertaining Pulaski; Mr. Thoggosh had given orders to Aelbraugh Pritsch that they weren't to be disturbed unless the asteroid was exploding (and added a footnote to admit Eichra Oren when he showed up).

Enjoying a respite, the nautiloid lifted a resigned tentacle. "I'm aware that your services are costly, Eichra Oren—don't belabor the fact. Let it stand that it's preferable to the more dangerous and costly alternative of transporting you back home. With these Americans, I can't predict how soon I'll require your talents again, perish the thought. I assume you're spending as much time with them as possible."

The man nodded. "For all the good it does either of us. The benefit of knowing more about events on their Earth than, say, someone like Pulaski expects may be more theoretical than—"

"*Mr. Thoggosh!*" The precise, fussy voice was Aelbraugh Pritsch's, transmitted from his own nearby office. Feathered sapients cared even less for fluorocarbon bathing than furry ones. An image of the man-sized avian or dinosauroid (it amounted to the same thing) welled in Eichra Oren's mind as his employer shared the incoming signal. "Nannel Rab reports equipment failure at Site Seventeen. I'm afraid it's the drilling system again."

"I suspected as much," the nautiloid sighed, sending his limb for another beer. "Have Nannel Rab follow the procedure we discussed. Keep me informed." He turned to the man. "You say the benefit of such knowledge is only theoretical?"

"May be theoretical," Eichra Oren corrected. "Despite the volume and quality of our data, there is much I don't understand about these inscrutable Americans and possibly never will."

"I see. That was to be expected, wasn't it? They have a lifetime in which to comprehend their civilization, and many of them fail, even so. What, in particular, is troubling you?"

"Many things." The human thought for a moment. "Just one item from the inventory as an example: where do the Chinese really fit into the current world political picture?"

"The formidable People's Republic." Mr. Thoggosh took a long drink. "You're acquiring personal reason to be curious?" He transmitted another deep and—his organs of respiration and speech having no connection—artificial sigh.

"You humans are irrepressible; no wonder there are ten billion of them on this Earth alone. What an experience, to spend one's life swimming in a fog of hormones, gripped by perpetual coupling frenzy."

Sam would have asked if it were envy speaking; he may even have suggested that Mr. Thoggosh couple himself. Eichra Oren gritted his teeth and ignored the gibe. "I've asked about them because I feel they're important. They've maintained a collectivist dictatorship for a century, murderous and repressive even by Marxist standards, but have a longer history of private capitalism which they show occasional interest in reviving. The World Soviet's afraid of that. They keep the massive Chinese population within their borders by brandishing the dirtiest nuclear weapons their science can devise. This encourages the Chinese to revert to an isolation they've been inclined toward readily enough on their own for thousands of years."

Eichra Oren was about to add something when Aelbraugh Pritsch filled their minds again. "I deplore interrupting, sir. Remgar d'Nod wishes to reduce power twenty-three percent while the matter-energy converter is serviced."

Had he been human, Mr. Thoggosh might have rubbed a hand across his face. The tip of one tentacle made small circles in the thin layer of sand beside his working area. "May I assume that this is not another equipment failure?"

"It's routine scheduled maintenance," the avian answered.

A tentacle slapped the sand pattern away in irritation. "Then why in the Predecessors' name does he bother me with it?" His tone changed as he cut the circuit and turned his attention again to Eichra Oren. "And the beautiful Rosalind Nguyen has nothing to do with this?" The mollusc possessed no eyebrows to raise skeptically at his employee, but managed to convey the impression anyway. "Perhaps not. She's of Vietnamese, rather than Chinese, extraction, isn't she?"

Again the man controlled himself, not without a struggle. An American habit he found particularly satisfying was their penchant for referring to an antagonist in terms of the terminal anatomical feature of the gastrointestinal system. Every sapient he knew of—excepting rare representatives of the plant kingdom—possessed such a feature. The epithet could be appreciated universally. He predicted a brilliant future for it among those compelled to associate with the Elders.

Again Aelbraugh Pritsch interrupted. "Sir, I have a report of two humans wandering near the abandoned boring platform at Site Four." Eichra Oren had been occupied with other matters, but recalled this as another location where subsurface geology had proven too much for nautiloid technology. Not for the first time, he wondered what they were drilling for.

"Was the excavation sealed?" his employer inquired.

"No, sir." Dinosauroid eyes rolled to an unseen ceiling, consulting organic memory or an electronic implant. "The crew was pulled off to another site. I'm sending a remote to see whether the bore collapsed on its own—unlikely in this gravity—or whether the humans might have discovered anything from examining the site." The remote, Eichra Oren knew, would be an aerostat like the one that had brought Pulaski, under cybernetic guidance without pilot or passengers.

"Let me know," came his employer's weary reply. "And Aelbraugh Pritsch?"

"Sir?" The bird-being's down-rimmed eyes widened, pupils contracting and expanding as he gave the nautiloid his worried attention.

"Try to relax, my feathered friend. Even the end of the world isn't the end of the world. See whether you can find out who these humans were. That might tell us something."

Visibly attempting, with little success, to follow Mr. Thoggosh's advice, he nodded. "I'll try, sir." Again his image faded from their minds.

"We were speaking," the nautiloid observed, "of China."

Eichra Oren lifted a hand. "All Dr. Nguyen says is, 'We don't talk about China,' 'we' meaning citizens of the American Soviet Socialist Republic, the Union of Soviet Socialist Republics, and the United World Soviet."

"Why do majoritarians give their nation-states such awkward names?'' Mr. Thoggosh mused. ''What was wrong with 'France' or even 'Bulgaria'? Never mind, please go on.''

''She's ethnically Chinese, like many twentieth-century Vietnamese who fled the oncoming wave. In the end, they only escaped from one variety of repression into another, but perhaps because of her background, she appears to have difficulty fitting in among her fellow Soviet Americans.''

''And as the sole non-Soviet human here,'' Mr. Thoggosh suggested, ''not to mention the only member of your species in our little group, you've developed more than a casual interest, is that it?''

The man frowned at what he felt was becoming a pattern of intrusion into his personal life. ''You could say that.''

''What is it this time?'' His employer was speaking with the disembodied voice of Aelbraugh Pritsch again.

''Nek Nam'l Las in Logistics. They can't find sixteen pallets of extra boring coolant we brought with us, and equipment failures have consumed more than planned. They want permission to send for more.''

Mr. Thoggosh was more than annoyed. ''What does that pebble counter think the transporter is, a tenthbit trolley? I discussed this with Nannel Rab and the other department heads yesterday, and thought it understood that we'll make do with what we have! Those pallets were moved from the equipment yard when space was required to disassemble the driver core damaged at Site Eleven. I knew some idiot would report them lost. They're stacked in the vehicle charge-and-storage bay at the north end of the converter. Tell Remgar d'Nod to move them back. Tell Nek Nam'l Las and everyone else there'll be no sending or receiving anything for another thousand hours! Turn down all such requests on your initiative. And one more thing, Aelbraugh Pritsch.''

The dinosauroid gulped. Not only were his pupils bouncing from half to twice their normal diameter with each heartbeat, but ruffled feathers around his neck made him look as if he were molting. Reminded of his assistant's physiological sensitivity, Mr. Thoggosh moderated his tone. "See here, I realized there hasn't been time for your remote to arrive at Site Four yet. Has Tl*m*nch*l managed to identify those wandering humans?" Tl*m*nch*l, whose name most sapients found unpronounceable, was an evolutionary relative of sea scorpions and Mr. Thoggosh's chief of security.

"No, sir, he's trying a cyberscan-and-match." The avian's feathers were smoother now. "But he complains that all humans look alike."

Mr. Thoggosh chuckled. "Only fair, I suppose, since I'm sure his people all look alike to humans. They certainly do to me. Now hold all messages, if you please, while I finish my conversation with Eichra Oren."

Aelbraugh Pritsch blinked—"Yes, sir"—and faded.

Visibly preparing to issue more orders, the mollusc appeared to inhale and exhale deeply. "Eichra Oren: I sympathize with your resentment of my personal remarks, just as I admire the romantic inclination every human I've ever known seems continuously inspired to manifest. I'd prefer that you forget Dr. Nguyen, although she intrigues you. Concentrate on Toya Pulaski, who is in a better position—something I doubt she realizes—to endanger a future triumph which will vindicate all past defeats."

"What do you mean, 'concentrate'?" There was more in what the nautiloid had said that worried Eichra Oren, but this would do for the moment.

Mr. Thoggosh lifted a tentacle. "Discover her likes and dislikes. Given her presumed heritage, normally I'd guess that she despises the current regime more than most; it's our misfortune that politics fail to interest her. We know she gave up her real love, paleontology, when drafted by the AeroSpace Force. Here among sapient molluscs, sea scorpions, dinosauroids, and others, she must have trouble deciding whether she's in a waking nightmare or has gone to her personal idea of heaven. I'd hazard that it offers features of both." He curled the limb into a sort of fist. "Stimulate her political uncertainty. Win her over, if you can, to our point of view.''

Eichra Oren's mouth compressed into a hard line. ''Fine, if I had a clue what our point of view is. Is this a professional assignment?'' He rose, clenching his own fists, determined to walk out.

''Sit down, Eichra Oren. I thought you understood that you were on the payroll the moment you arrived and will remain so as long as you're here, in whatever capacity. Knowing humans as I do, I'm aware that Toya happens to be, by your aesthetic standards as well as those of her own culture, an unlovely thing. Although you'd gallantly have it otherwise, this makes what I ask all the more difficult. Be that as it may, due to her interest in paleontology, she represents a threat to an achievement which will make good all our past shortcomings. She must be turned aside. If you wish to add a surcharge, if it will make the task any less unsavory, by all means do so.''

Eichra Oren stood beside the chair. Only at a time like this did it occur to him how small and frail human beings must look, how ridiculous he must appear, confronting a creature ten times his mass with dozens of powerful tentacles meters long. ''Before you change your mind about what profession I'm here to practice, consider my lack of credentials in the field, instead of haggling over the price!''

''This is American humor?'' Mr. Thoggosh asked mildly.

Disgusted with his lack of dignity (Eichra Oren was capable of winning a physical battle with a nautiloid and had done so as a professional necessity), he stepped around the chair and sat again, arms folded across his chest, mind seething with suspicion. ''Better than nautiloid humor, hiring me to protect your little secret and not telling me what I'm supposed to protect.''

''We come to it at last!'' Mr. Thoggosh laughed. ''Dear boy, I acknowledge that you're stranded here as a result of a task I hired you to accomplish, one I confess you performed with astonishing alacrity, in a manner satisfactory to me.

I'm obliged to see that you suffer no further for it, just as I would if you'd been injured in the line of duty.'' Apparently surprised to find his container empty again, he sent his tentacle for another, bringing the coffee Eichra Oren preferred without asking. Knowing his employer, the man accepted it as the token of reconciliation it was meant to be.

''It's your fortune,'' he continued, ''good or ill, that you're free as a kind of workman's compensation to enjoy this time as a vacation if you wish, with no additional obligation. It's my fortune, and I regard it unreservedly as good, that you're not a man to whom idleness for its own sake is welcome. I'm grateful you're willing to help me perform my solemn duty, even at the confiscatory rates you deserve.''

Eichra Oren did have eyebrows, and raised them. ''But?''

''You ask too much. If the Americans—or worse, their *leader*—were to discover what we seek here, not learn what it is but make the find before us, it would culminate in a disaster of unparalleled magnitude.''

''If it's so serious, I'd like to help. You're willing to swear Scutigera to secrecy. I'm your friend, I'm Eneri Relda's son, I'm a *p'Nan* assessor for reason's sake! Why won't you confide in me?''

Mr. Thoggosh thought long before answering. ''I need partners like Scutigera; it can't be helped. I chose them as best I could. Even so, each morning I awaken hoping I've chosen wisely.''

''I have some savings—make me a partner.''

''Eichra Oren, I esteem your discretion above that of any sapient I know, excepting your mother. At this point, I wouldn't confide in her. The risk is unthinkable. If you wish to help—and for the sake of restitution which will pay for every past transgression we ever made against ourselves, I hope you do—distract and occupy the attentions of Toya Pulaski!''

IX
Shadow among Shadows

Arthur Empleado was cold.

He hadn't thought it possible in these artificial tropics. Orbiting 390 million kilometers from the sun, 5023 Eris was a hothouse, every centimeter of the false upper surface provided by her biological canopy given to absorbing and hoarding sunlight. Yet he was chilled to numbness, almost to the bone.

It was conceivable that what he felt had less to do with temperature than with his exclusion from the group lounging around the campfire in the center of the hollow formed by the three shuttles. It was never stated in so many words (no one would have dared, even given their isolation from Earth and the disrespect habitually shown by the mission's highest ranking officers), but as principal KGB agent, charged with maintaining ideological consistency, he wasn't welcome socially among the other personnel and he knew it.

On the other hand he was used to it. A likelier source of his present discomfort was the paper slip he fingered in his jacket pocket, a note left in his bunk earlier today. Now that he considered it, just the thought caused him to ache and shiver, shifting from one foot to the other in the shadows, watching his shipmates enjoy each other's company in a way forbidden to him not only by current circumstances, but a lifetime's habit and inclination.

dam oooo: wound my heart with monotonous langour

Ironically, he'd selected the code himself eighteen months ago, expecting to hear it someday planted in a transmission from Earth, never anticipating that he'd be reading it hand-scrawled in ballpoint on a scrap little larger than a postage stamp. The historic phrase, lifted from an obscure poem and broadcast by the BBC one hundred years ago, had informed French partisans, mostly good Communists like himself, that the long night of Fascist domination was about to end with the Allied invasion of Normandy. For him it meant orders were coming from the American KGB that would override every other duty and obligation. Assigned to the expedition as a civilian, he'd secretly been commissioned as an ASF general officer, the microfilmed documentation he carried dated retroactively to give him seniority over Gutierrez in the emergency that would constitute his only justification for revealing it.

He examined the gathering around the campfire with renewed professional interest. Among these unlikely candidates (and several others not present at this evening's festivities) who was his likeliest contact?

Lieutenant Colonel Juan Sebastiano was rather young to be commander—Empleado was annoyed at the untidiness of referring to a colonel as "captain"—of the *Metzenbaum* or of anything else important. Empleado had always rated him politically unreliable. He had a careless mouth with regard to authority and was personally loyal to Gutierrez. Empleado cherished plans for dealing with him when time and opportunity presented themselves. The same evident qualities might make a perfect cover. Still, Empleado had a feeling for these things. He couldn't see Sebastiano as any sort of agent.

Major Jesus Ortiz was a different matter. It was said the new commander of the *Wright* had ancestors, not that remote, who thought it hilarious to skin the soles of a victim's feet and let him walk home across a broiling desert floor. He remembered reading that the Apaches and Comanches were afraid of the Yaquis. Of course the rumor might be untrue. Empleado's personnel files, abbreviated for space-flight, didn't go back that far. And Ortiz may not have inherited his forebears' sense of humor. That sort of san-guine ruthlessness wasn't the best test of a good agent, anyway. Empleado himself had a rather tender stomach when it came to the brute mechanics of interrogation, a failing he tried to make up for in other ways. Nevertheless, it wouldn't surprise him if his contact turned out to be Ortiz.

Someone else with an equivalent rank of major was his own subordinate, Roger Betal. The man was becoming a problem, his usefulness destroyed by a beating at the hands of this interloper Eichra Oren and what had happened to his fellow enforcers Roo and Hake. Empleado had relied not only on Betal's martial arts, but his ability as a deceptively charming talker. Surprisingly, that ability was always less effective with female subjects than expected. Now he seemed to be avoiding Empleado, seeking the company of expeditionaries friendly with the so-called Elders and their pet human. Such a problem was best dealt with sooner than later—unless the whole thing was a brilliant ruse and Betal was the one who'd left the note in his bunk.

Empleado shook his head. This game he'd begun playing with himself was useless. The next person he considered was Rosalind Nguyen. As a physician, she was an ideal intelligence gatherer. Women were, especially small, pretty ones. She saw crew members in their weakest moments and most vulnerable states of mind. Carrying the rank of captain lent her a measure of nonintimidating authority while her ethnic origin, the political background it implied, might lead them to believe she'd be sympathetic with their discontents, since she was ideologically suspect simply by being what she was. He'd never say that the government of the ASSR was racist—not within hearing of his superiors and at the same time hope to continue occupying a position within that government himself. It was wise to avoid the habit of even thinking it too frequently. But one look at personnel distribution, at the disproportionate number of Hispanics and blacks and their relative ranks within the AeroSpace Force, would convince anyone it was more fashionable these days to possess certain surnames than others or to lay claim to certain ancestors.

Someone passed a guitar to First Lieutenant Lee Marna, life-support tech for the *Metzenbaum*. She let her fingers ripple across the nylon strings, singing of "the strangest dream I never had before." There was an amazing number of amateur musicians with the expedition. If it were within his power, he'd have forbidden it. A guitar was worse than a loaded gun. Homemade music, like homemade humor, was inherently subversive, especially made by an attractive young woman whose corn-silk hair and fair complexion, opposing the officially encouraged fashion he'd been thinking about earlier, drew attention to the performance. In the interests of state security, entertainment must be left to carefully winnowed specialists. He'd always argued that the greatest danger to authority was laughter (any unsanctioned happiness, for that matter), which the state could not provide as a reward for approved behavior and was not therefore in a position to deny as a punishment.

Empleado wasn't the only one watching the little blond appreciatively. Second Lieutenant Danny Gutierrez—now there was a thought: what if the general's son were the undercover agent? What did he know about the boy? He was Gutierrez's second son. The eldest had been killed in some particularly horrible manner during a recent unpublicized conflict in southern Africa. Danny was a friend of Sebastiano's, to appearances more the colonel's protégé than his father's. That placed him in position to keep an eye on Sebastiano, provided anyone in power felt the colonel were important enough to merit it. Or it might just represent precaution on the general's part. Like racism, nepotism wasn't unknown within the ASSR, but blatancy was a greater failing. Young Gutierrez was a petty criminal, a smuggler and small dealer in forbidden goods. That would provide him with credentials.

Whatever his status, it was obvious the boy might soon have another problem on his hands, and only on his hands if he were lucky. He hadn't noticed the longing glances cast his way by Demene Wise, making a first appearance in public since Eichra Oren had crippled one of his knees, possibly for life. Before the mishap, Wise had been another of Empleado's informal staff with the equivalent rank of Master Sergeant. Empleado, preserving the tatters of his cover, hadn't visited him in the improvised sick bay and didn't know whether he'd show an inclination, like Betal, to avoid his superior. With his great cube of a head and enormous shoulders, he still looked carved from basalt. Judging from his sagging face, he'd aged twenty years. The man had never seemed particularly bright, but in his present frame of mind, Empleado considered Wise's perversion as possible KGB cover without rejecting it altogether. His presence in the gathering was being tolerated, possibly for the doctor's sake. Aside from a quality of his body language which contrasted with his Herculean appearance, and his effeminate mooning over the general's son, he seemed to be enjoying the music as much as anyone.

As Marna played, firelight picked out the dark, bearded features of Staff Sergeant C. C. Jones, former TV star, now eyes and ears for *American Truth* and, rumor had it, enemy of Horatio Gutierrez. Empleado wished he knew more about that. He always wished he knew more about everything. As usual, Jones was trying to steal the scene, lending conspicuous approval to whatever everyone else demonstrated they were enjoying, in this case, the lieutenant's singing.

Of the many types for which he had nothing but contempt, journalists held top position on Empleado's list, even above politicians. Anyone, from left to right, who'd ever been personally connected with an event that became news knew they were incapable of getting the simplest story straight. Pre–Soviet American journalism had always gloried in its self-appointed role as watchdog over the rights of the individual. The truth was that during its long, self-congratulatory history, it had been more like a cur caught bloody-muzzled time after time, savaging the very flocks it was trusted to protect.

No one knew better than the KGB that there was no such thing as "the news." Jones, his colleagues, and his predecessors peddled gossip, mostly in the form of horrible things happening to faraway strangers, things that might have happened to *you* and still might, unless . . . More ignorant than the twelve-year-old minds they pitched to, dirtier than the ward heelers they kept an eye on, they were merchants of fear, parasites nourishing on calamities that bred more fear and an ever more powerful state which grew by promising to keep everybody safe from everything. Since the universe is inherently unsafe, it was a profitable symbiosis. They might single out this incompetent bureaucrat or that corrupt politician, they might favor those whose paranoia dwelt on domestic danger rather than foreign, but they never questioned the paranoia itself or the wisdom of erecting a security state to assuage it. They never took the individual's side against the growth of power.

Empleado approved of the security state and recognized the importance of journalists in creating and maintaining it. That didn't make associating with them turn his stomach any less.

Reflected firelight from Pulaski's glasses caught his eye, distracting him. The idea that this gangly, bespectacled female—what was the old-fashioned word?—this *nerd* might be a high-ranking undercover operative for the KGB was so ridiculous he refused to consider it.

For similar reasons, he rejected machinist Corporal Roger Owen. His own father, Salvador, had been a machinist, dragging himself home with blackened nails, reeking of overheated solvents, slouching in a dilapidated armchair swilling rationed beer while Arturo's *mamacita* fried the evening tortillas and beans, watching TV propaganda as if it meant something. How the old man's son had longed to get out of that house, however well it reflected the proletarian ideal, out of that self-consciously blue-collar life, to do something that would leave his hands clean after a day's work, to get a glimpse of what lay behind the propaganda, to make something important of himself.

It wasn't that he hadn't loved them in his way. Father like son was an ardent if naive Marxist, loyal to his union and the socialism it buttressed only slightly less solidly than journalism. But Empleado distrusted men who worked with their hands. They were too bound up in the concretes of life, unable to detach themselves from petty facts. They insisted that philosophy and politics make sense—dollars and cents—unable to see that nobody interested in accruing power had anything to gain by limiting himself to the mundane. Besides, he thought, if Owen had written the note, it would have been in soft pencil with greasy thumbprints around the edges.

As Marna finished her song, Rubber Chicken Alvarez, last and by any measure least of the group around the fire, became the life of the party, telling jokes he laughed loudest at himself. In other circumstances he'd have been wearing a lampshade; Empleado was confident these would-be Robinson Crusoes would be weaving him one next week out of bean sprouts or whatever the corporal was cooking in his cast-iron pot. If he'd had to stake his life on it, Empleado believed he'd bet on Carlos the Clown, preparer of food, disposer of garbage, maker of practical jokes, as his KGB spy. He fit the role of community idiot too perfectly. He played the fool too well.

dam oooo: wound my heart with monotonous langour

It could only mean "the dam at midnight." Glancing at his watch, he slipped from the camp headed for his rendezvous. It didn't take him long to get there. "Dam" was an ambitious term for the barrier of meteoric stone (carbonaceous chondrite, which comprised most of the asteroid, was too crumbly) piled across the stream where it came nearest the camp. The idea was to raise the level to obtain running water. Sebastiano, who'd taken charge of the project, still hadn't any idea what he was going to use for pipes—plastic provided by the Elders or hollow trunks of bamboolike plants.

The site had been chosen for more than proximity. Here also the stream passed through a gully which, once full, would make a natural reservoir. The gully itself was probably a deformed impact crater, a random feature of terrain which had never been shaped by moving air or water until the Elders had recently created an atmosphere. At the moment, the dam was less than a meter high—Sebastiano's men were having to go farther afield in search of suitable rocks to add to it—and the water less than half that depth.

Empleado heard a noise, turned, and was blinded by intense light. In the next heartbeat, someone was standing beside him turning a small black knurled aluminum flashlight downward to shine on the thin slip of plastic that served each expedition member as ID and—with information-retrieval equipment—a dossier on the person it was issued to. This one was unique, its back surface consisting of a hologram. Seeming to float above the card was the curved, elaborate shield of the KGB.

"Satisfied, Comrade?" came a whispered voice.

"You!" Empleado couldn't help gasping.

X
Prostitution

Eichra Oren looked around at the audience gathered in the clearing.

"This morning," he told them, "if there's no objection, I'll communicate in the human language English for the benefit of those without augmentation. Please adjust your implants to the appropriate translation channel."

The *p'Nan* debt assessor sat cross-legged on a blanket at the base of a huge canopy tree, his sword lying across his knees. Sam lay nearby, tongue out, looking like an ordinary dog. Overhead and to the rear, the pearlescent fungoid growth that would soon be Eichra Oren's quarters jutted over the nearby stream. For a few seconds only the murmur of that stream broke the silence as sapients of many sizes and shapes briefly contemplated an inner reality unshared, *as yet*, the thought entered Toya's mind, by the small handful of humans present.

They were a mixed handful as well, increasingly uncaring of position or rank. Betal was here, having appointed himself a sort of follower to the Antarctican. The general, behaving self-consciously toward her as he had since last night, sat beside her on a convenient fallen log. His son Danny leaned against a tree across the clearing, conversing with Sebastiano until the moment Eichra Oren spoke. Not far away, Ortiz glowered (that being his natural, relaxed expression) either at Wise, here for a therapeutic outing on his crippled knee, his doctor (and everyone else's) Rosalind Nguyen, or at C. C. Jones, whom none of the officers seemed to like although Toya thought him handsome with his rugged features and salt-and-pepper beard. In the middle of the clearing, surrounded by aliens, sat Owen and Marna. Even Rubber Chicken Alvarez had shown up. What interest that overgrown class clown had in these proceedings defied Toya's power of imagination. The only individual she missed was Empleado, and she didn't miss him much.

Aside from her own cosapients, it seemed to her that no two creatures among Eichra Oren's listeners were of the same species. Until a moment ago—the same moment Danny had quit talking—Dlee Raftan Saon, courtly surgeon of an insectile race, had been enjoying what may have been a professional discussion with Rosalind, although Toya rather doubted it. Raftan liked the ladies—of whatever species—and had once even ''kissed'' Toya's hand.

Llessure Knarrfic was here too, which Toya found surprising since that individual was a busy executive in Mr. Thoggosh's various enterprises and on top of that, a sort of potted plant-being resembling a giant rubber flower.

Remaulthiek, on the other hand, dispensed refreshments at Dlee Raftan Saon's infirmary. She resembled a big gray quilt in a plastic bag, being distantly related to skates and rays. She was always interested in anything to do with moral indebtedness. Her rather menial vocation was something of a penance she had long ago imposed on herself for some unknown transgression.

There was no sign of the sea scorpions who provided security here, nor of Aelbraugh Pritsch, Mr. Thoggosh's assistant, nor of the Proprietor (as Aelbraugh Pritsch referred to him) himself. Scutigera was rumored to be off on the other side of the asteroid, dealing with some technical problem which had been bedeviling the nautiloids. Toya did see a giant spider, three meters tall and strikingly beautiful in its red and sable furry pelt.

After a moment, Eichra Oren nodded. ''Before we begin, let me help our guests understand what's about to happen. As many of you appreciate, the one debt assessment they've seen was unusual and may have given them a false impression of what takes place under normal circumstances.''

He shifted on his blanket, settling into a more comfortable position.

''For most of human history, disputes between individuals have been settled by professional arbiters paid by a government which they—the arbiters—rely on to impose whatever decisions they arrive at, by coercive physical force. Which is to say by threat of injury or death. Those among you unfamiliar with the concept of government will find it described among human customs on the supplementary information channels.''

For reasons Toya could only guess, a mild disturbance

sifted through the crowd. Eichra Oren let it fade before continuing. "Irrational assumptions, faulty logic, and politically expedient dispositions are the hallmark of such an arrangement. Trial by ordeal was common throughout many human cultures. Imperial magistrates in ancient China were legally empowered to torture testimony from unwilling witnesses, even those not criminally accused. It was left, I imagine, to a magistrate's personal integrity whether that process produced anything resembling the truth."

Another stir and Toya knew her guess had been correct. The nonhumans were scandalized at this description of human customs while the humans, feeling they were being slandered, reacted in a similar manner. Eichra Oren gave his listeners a moment to absorb the horror of what he'd told them. Meanwhile the nearby stream did more to preserve the resulting silence than to break it, its minimal white noise muffling other sounds.

"Greater individuation, however," Eichra Oren resumed at last, "is the inviolable rule of evolution. No despot, however draconian, has ever been entirely successful at stopping it. Over many centuries, the brute power of these false arbiters—'judges' they were called—came to be limited and more or less objective standards of evidence and procedure adopted. By the current civilization's nineteenth century, due to worldwide majoritarian influence, judges were generally held to be servants of the people. Even some of them believed it. Everyone involved pretended not to notice where their salaries came from and the conflict of interest this represented."

Absently, he turned his sword up to rest on its scabbard-tip. "What was called the 'rule of law'—meaning participation in the process by government, an entity beyond reach of any law—distorted and contaminated every honest effort to balance the moral scales. While this illustrates one of many dangers inherent in authority, what counts is that for a time, judges no longer appeared to wield absolute power in the name of some ruler, but nominally on behalf of those they were presumed to serve. However ephemeral and illusory it proved, the difference may turn out to have been philosophically significant.''

He fixed his gaze on Toya or perhaps on Gutierrez sitting beside her. ''It isn't my intention to criticize the customs of our new acquaintances, but to clarify our own by contrast. Pragmatic or philosophical, any differences between those majoritarian judges and their predecessors evaporate, compared to those between them and myself. My clients come of their own volition, seeking the benefit of whatever knowledge and skill I possess. I've no power to compel their presence, nor the testimony of witnesses, nor acquiescence to any judgment I render. A culture in which people are forced to behave as if they were virtuous (however you define the term) can never know virtue, only sullen compliance and its concomitant, widespread, furtive criminality.''

Across the clearing, Danny laughed out loud.

''On the other hand,'' Eichra Oren told them, ''when an individual's fortune rises or falls with whatever virtue he spontaneously manifests, his culture discovers within him virtues neither he nor it suspected. My clients pay for my services themselves and these are the only conditions under which I can guarantee value. The power to compel would only make what I do harder, although it would be an easy way to cheat my customers, forcing them to accept the sight of my thumb on the scales of justice.''

Toya yawned, realizing that it was an inauspicious start on the task she'd been given the previous evening—early this morning, actually. It wasn't her fault that her superiors had kept her up half the night briefing her—after questioning her relentlessly about her conversation with Mr. Thoggosh—but she also realized that, whoever was really to blame, she'd be held responsible for any failure. She would certainly have never asked for this duty, as a *spy* of all things.

''I know it's a bizarre assignment I'm giving you, Pulaski.'' She hadn't believed what she was hearing. Leaning against one of the pilot's chairs, Gutierrez had hesitated, almost shy as he attempted to explain himself. *And he should be*, she'd thought, *considering what he's asking!* Her most heartfelt wish was the same as it had been since landing here, that they'd all just leave her alone to study the Elders and their odd companions.

Gutierrez had looked down at his hands. "I'm not certain I can legally order you to do it under ASF regulations."

"I can, Sergeant, I assure you." Empleado leaned forward in his lightweight folding chair, another of the Elders' puzzling gifts, emerging from an unlit corner of the command deck where he sat, listening. The agent took a final drag on his cigarette—like others, he'd recently succumbed and taken up the habit again—stubbing it out in an improvised ashtray turned out by Corporal Owen. "It's perfectly legal under KGB authority which, in case it escaped your attention, I happen to represent." He shook a finger at them. "That's the only consideration which should be important to either of you."

He sat back, his features indistinct again in the shadows. Through the windows, fireflies—a decorative domestic species someone had told her—with fat abdomens that made them the size of canaries twinkled at the edge of the jungle surrounding the encampment.

Gutierrez shook his head. "It's important to me, Art, that the sergeant understand why I—why we're giving her these orders." He returned to her. "There doesn't seem to be another choice. You know our situation, Toya, as well as anybody. You also know that Mr. Thoggosh is searching for something on this asteroid, more and more desperately, it appears to me. Perhaps we can make use of whatever he's looking for to get ourselves out of this mess."

Standing almost at attention, hard to do in the cramped conditions, she began to reply bitterly, "And I'm the only one you thought of—"

"I don't like it," he interrupted, showing her a palm, "and you may like it even less before it's over with. But we have to take advantage of the one card we've been dealt. You're in a unique position to find out what they're looking for, and I want you to do exactly that.''

Toya was frustrated. ''I don't know why you keep saying that, sir.''

''I'll spell it out. You've heard the rumor that Mr. Thoggosh is looking for some sort of fossil remains beneath the accretion crust.''

''Yes, sir, from two of the *Metzenbaum* crew who spent all day yesterday poking around one of the abandoned drilling sites until an unmanned flying machine ran them off.''

''Toya, you're the only one who'd recognize the significance of such a find if you happened across it.'' He hesitated, his words coming slowly, as if he were ashamed of them. ''The easiest way is probably through Eichra Oren. Given what happened with Reille y Sanchez, he may be emotionally vulnerable right now, susceptible—''

Empleado leaned forward again, eagerly. ''You must expend *every possible effort*, Sergeant, to determine what this Antarctican knows!''

Toya whirled, feeling the sudden heat of angry embarrassment rising in her face. ''You mean I'm supposed to try to seduce it out of him?'' She turned more slowly this time, to face the general. ''Is that right?''

Gutierrez didn't answer, perhaps thinking the question had been directed at Empleado. The KGB man, understanding that it hadn't been, that it was more of an appeal than a question, stepped in. ''Tell her, General,'' he insisted, ''that she must do more than just try.''

Gutierrez shook his head. Gazing out the window into the darkness, he talked almost to himself. ''I keep imagining how I'd feel if I learned one of my daughters had been ordered to—''

''Prostitute herself for the State?'' Empleado laughed unpleasantly. ''What higher purpose could a woman serve, especially one like her?'' He observed her with a sneer, ostensibly addressing his remarks to Gutierrez. "You merely want her to understand, General. I wish to leave absolutely nothing to her imagination. I'm relying on you to help: she is to do whatever it takes to accomplish her mission. Isn't that so?"

Empleado seemed to be enjoying himself. The general's face was still turned away, his attention somewhere outside the window. But he'd nodded, confirming the edict.

What they weren't telling her, she'd realized with a sinking heart, was how to go about transforming her rather drab self from the bespectacled nerd she knew herself to be into something resembling a Mata Hari.

XI
Restitution

"Now then, who requires my services first?"

Like Pulaski and a handful of others, Gutierrez was among those drawn the next morning by an announcement of Eichra Oren's first public session as a *p'Nan* assessor. Moral debt had been much on the general's mind the past few days, especially the past few hours, especially in connection with the amateur paleontologist. He knew she was unhappy with the assignment he and Empleado had imposed on her. What she didn't know, what thousands of years of military tradition would never have allowed him to tell her, was that he despised himself for giving her the order.

"I do, Eichra Oren."

Something flowed from an edge of the crowd. Gutierrez's

first impression was of a human stick-figure rendered in red-orange pipe cleaners with an extra leg standing in place of its head. His second, a product of hundreds of nature documentaries watched with half an eye and half a mind, was of a deep-sea brittle starfish with long, sinuous arms and a ceramic-looking pentagonal "torso" where the arms met. Its voice was human enough, even pleasant.

As with those TV shows, the general's mind was elsewhere, still focused on Pulaski. However reluctantly, he was acting on secret orders of his own direct from the American KGB through a watcher-of-watchers code-named "Iron Butterfly," officially unknown to him until minutes before the meeting with Toya. "Officially" was a flexible word: Gutierrez had made it his business from the first premission training day to know his people, including the backup undercover agent charged with keeping an eye on the expedition's overt political officer, Empleado, as well as its first-string covert operative, Richardson. What Gutierrez hadn't realized until now was that it was also Iron Butterfly's job to report to the Banker on the everyday activities and attitudes of the thirty-odd surviving "heroes" of the expedition.

"Very well," the debt assessor replied, "and you are?"

The creature approached on two of its delicate limbs and suddenly relaxed onto the ground beside him. "I'm Clym Pucras."

"Greetings, Clym Pucras." Eichra Oren entwined arms with it and released it. "Will you tell me your profession?"

"I'm a machine-tool designer."

Gutierrez also knew (never mind how, he thought) that Iron Butterfly was a bitter, twisted spirit. Contrary to the agent's official—and completely phony—background story, Iron Butterfly's homeland was a Caribbean satellite that had almost broken free from Russian influence just before America had willingly adopted Marxism, spoiling everything for the little island nation. That this should make Iron Butterfly a more zealous instrument of Soviet policy didn't make a lot of sense, but it was a common, very human reaction, reflecting a certain vindictive fatalism.

"Would you describe yourself," Eichra Oren went on, "as a sovereign individual of fully intact sapience?"

Clym Pucras lifted a tentacle and splayed the tip into a five-fingered hand. "Without undue modesty, I would."

"Does anyone dispute this?" The man lifted his eyes to the crowd. The muttering of a single individual—another starfish-creature—arose and died without any real dispute being offered.

The general had every confidence that Empleado's sources kept him aware of Iron Butterfly's machinations. He regarded Empleado as a tolerable moderate, unmoved by any humanitarian spirit but by physical squeamishness which produced the same results. The tragedy (for the expedition, anyway) was that to keep himself above suspicion, he must now pursue his job with a zeal—and cruelty—he wouldn't otherwise have exhibited.

"That being established," Eichra Oren returned to his client, "where do you live, Clym Pucras?"

The creature waved a limb again, part of its body language, Gutierrez guessed. "I presently make my home on the south side of the uppermost branch level of the third tree west of the matter-energy converter."

"Within the Elders' Settlement on the asteroid known as 5023 Eris?"

"Yes, that's correct."

Thus, between them, Iron Butterfly, to whom brutality came naturally, and Empleado, fearful and ambitious, had already combined to make life miserable for Pulaski. Gutierrez feared she was only the first such victim.

"So much for formalities," came the reply. "What can I do for you?"

Clym Pucras rose a centimeter or so, turned slightly, and resettled himself. Or herself, the general thought. Or itself. "I request that you render an assessment with regard to appropriate restitution, inasmuch as I've recently trespassed against the physical property of one Babnap Portycel, creating on my part a state of moral indebtedness to him.''

"You committed this trespass willfully," Eichra Oren raised his eyebrows, "against that being's plainly expressed wishes to the contrary?''

"I'm afraid I did." Clym Pucras's limbs drooped.

"Babnap Portycel is also a resident of the Settlement on 5023 Eris?''

"Yes," Clym Pucras answered, "also on the third tree west of the matter-energy converter, on the south side of uppermost branch level—save one."

The assessor looked at the crowd again. "Is Babnap Portycel here today?''

"He is," Clym Pucras told him.

Eichra Oren showed a palm. "Let's have him answer for himself. Babnap Portycel, will you identify yourself? Are you present?''

The former mutterer arose on wiry limbs. "Reluctantly, Eichra Oren.''

"Wait a minute." Pulaski turned to the general, whispering. "It's the trespasser, not the property owner, who's bringing suit? Against himself?''

"Shhh!" Gutierrez answered impatiently.

Not having heard the byplay, Eichra Oren went on. "Your reluctance is noted. Clym Pucras, one more question before we begin. Do you object to assessment being rendered in public, as an example to our human guests?''

"Not at all," answered the starfish-creature. "I intended it to be exemplary. I'd be honored.''

Pulaski whispered again. "What does he mean, 'begin'? This character has already admitted to the crime. What else is left but the sentence?''

"Shhh!" replied Gutierrez, the same as before.

"All right, Clym Pucras, you might start by telling me about the trespass in your own words. Try to be brief, but I want the whole story.''

As if struggling against its own weight, it tilted itself until the pentagonal portion of its body, now diagonal, could be seen. "Gladly. I was pacing the balcony of my dwelling yesternoon, preoccupied with the repeated failure of certain plasma drills I had designed for Mr. Thoggosh, when I missed my step—I'm not quite sure what happened—and fell over the rail. My species are somewhat frail of constitution compared to others—I make no excuse, mind you—and a fall of that distance to the ground would certainly have killed me. I took the only chance I had and seized the rail of Babnap Portycel's balcony as I passed it, one branch level below."

"I see," Eichra Oren told the creature, "please go on."

"Babnap Portycel saw me from within. He rushed out complaining that I was on his property without permission and demanded that I let go the rail."

"In order to fall to your death." Gutierrez knew Eichra Oren well enough by now to see that he was suppressing some facial expression, although he wasn't sure which. "I gather you didn't."

"I considered it, letting go the rail, thinking I might stop my fall again on the next level below. But by that time I had grown fatigued and feared I might not be able to save myself that way twice. As I say, I make no excuse for my unprincipled behavior."

"That, too, is noted," observed the man, "although I suggest you leave final judgment to me. You're paying me to make it. What did you do?"

Clym Pucras gave a shrug. "I pulled myself onto his balcony, entered his dwelling, and made my exit in a conventional manner, by the spiral staircase which services all the dwellings on that tree."

"I see. Did Babnap Portycel resist you, either when you pulled yourself over the rail or made your exit through his apartment?"

"No, and I'm grateful. He continued to complain bitterly. I acknowledge that he'd have been within his rights to push me off or shoot me."

"Indeed he would," Eichra Oren nodded. "Did you linger in his apartment or proceed straight to the door?"

"The latter. Babnap Portycel's rather shrill voice was giving me pain in my auditory organs—although I concede he was well within his rights."

Eichra Oren looked up. "Babnap Portycel—you needn't rise—has Clym Pucras accurately described what happened yesterday?"

Gutierrez happened to be closer to this member of the species and had a better view of it. Neither seemed to be wearing the transparent plastic moisture suits affected by many aquatic species, but they did speak through thin-film sound transducers affixed to their carapaces.

"He had, Eichra Oren, although now the damage is done, I wish he hadn't bothered! He violated my rights! I don't want his restitution!"

"I don't suppose you do, Babnap Portycel." Eichra Oren's voice was suddenly weary, as if he'd heard it all a thousand times. "I suspect you'd find it far more satisfying to have him remain in your moral debt the rest of his life. Well, as an assessor of the *p'Nan* school, I can't permit that, and I won't. Civilization rests on the ability and willingness of individuals to pay their moral debts to one another."

Babnap Portycel made a snorting noise which, despite his utterly alien shape, reminded Gutierrez of Grumpy from *Snow White*.

"Now, Clym Pucras," Eichra Oren continued, "ordinarily I wouldn't ask this question and you're certainly not obliged to answer, but our guests may find what you have to say enlightening. If Babnap Portycel doesn't want any restitution, why did you come to me?"

"I want my other neighbors to know that despite what I did to Babnap Portycel, I continue to respect their right to property and privacy, just as I respect his. I want them to understand that, like any decent individual, I'm willing to pay my debts in full, moral and otherwise. Also, Eichra

Oren, I'd rather not remain indebted to a curmudgeon like Babnap Portycel.''

This time the man couldn't resist a chuckle. "I can't say that I blame you. Anything else?"

"Now that you mention it. I feel self-conscious saying this in the presence of a famous debt assessor who deals with this sort of thing every day, but I was concerned about the precedent that might be set by Babnap Portycel's refusal to accept restitution.''

"Nor can we force him, since that would establish a worse precedent. On this Earth it's called 'eminent domain.' But I believe I know what you mean. Would you mind explaining for our guests?''

The pentagonal shape with five sinuous tentacles sprouting from its sides swiveled to face Gutierrez. "Thinking afterward, I was deeply troubled. It had been an emergency, but my use of Babnap Portycel's property, if it were to become generally acceptable, would inevitably be abused. The time is long past when anyone who lives among the Elders asserts his need as a claim on the lives of others, as I gather is customary among humans. The word 'emergency' is subjective: people would begin cutting through a neighbor's property—mine, for example—merely for the sake of convenience. Such violations are habitual, progressive. Before long we'd be living like animals, reduced to the level of . . ." Clym Pucras swiveled toward Eichra Oren. "I can't remember the human expression.''

" 'Socialism','' stated the assessor, "and I fully agree. Your trespass was understandable in the circumstances and Babnap Portycel's refusal to help at least unkind. But as a human philosopher once observed, one's need doesn't constitute a mortgage on someone else's life. Babnap Portycel was not morally obligated to tolerate your presence, let alone help you.

"Now on one hand, the purpose of property rights in particular and moral codes in general is to support the lives of sapients. On the other, they must support the lives of the specific sapients they belong to or they're without meaning. You acted to preserve your life, something we can all sympathize with and, in a different context, even commend. However, should need become a general excuse for violating individual rights, all of our lives, in effect, would eventually be forfeit, defeating the whole reason for having moral codes in the first place. Your concern was well placed."

"Thank you, Eichra Oren."

He raised a hand. "Don't thank me yet. I also agree with your choice of words. Babnap Portycel is as curmudgeonly a being as I've heard of. That's his right. Curmudgeons, whether they intend it or not, do us all a favor. In many cultures, miners take birds into the earth to warn, through their fragile metabolism, of poison gas or lack of oxygen. Curmudgeons are their moral equivalent. A culture which fails to uphold the rights of curmudgeons, no matter how inconvenient, no matter how tempting it is to cut corners 'this once,' degenerates until no one has any rights, not even nice people.

"Now, Clym Pucras," asked the assessor, "how long would you estimate you occupied Babnap Portycel's property without his permission?"

"I'm not certain. Perhaps a minute, perhaps two."

"To be sure," declared Eichra Oren, "I advise you to offer him five minutes' rent on his rail, balcony, and dwelling at the most exorbitant rate being charged in that neighborhood. I estimate that this should come to five hundred copper sandgrains. Have you that much with you?"

"Yes, Eichra Oren, I believe I have." One tentacle held out five copper coins, another proffered a token of gold. "And enough to pay you, as well."

"You and I can settle later, Clym Pucras. Go ahead and pay him now."

Clym Pucras arose, approached Babnap Portycel who now sat alone in a clear area in the middle of the crowd, and offered him the copper coins. Babnap Portycel slapped them from his cosapient's manipulator.

"I told you, I don't want your money!"

Clym Pucras turned expectantly to Eichra Oren.

The assessor nodded. "You've done your best, Clym Pucras. Babnap Portycel has refused restitution in front of witnesses. Go home now and see whether the neighbors whose good opinion you value don't agree that the moral balance has been restored."

" 'Go thou'," Pulaski whispered, " 'and sin no more.' "

XII
Selfsame Seducers

Finished for the day, Eichra Oren watched his audience and clients depart the clearing in apparent varying degrees of perplexity or satisfaction, depending on whether they were human or members of another species. Once more he felt he'd failed to help the former understand the latter and had the whole task still before him to do over again.

Toward the opposite end of the little grassy spot, only Pulaski lingered, sitting at one end of the log she'd shared with Gutierrez, eyes downcast, fingers playing idly with a long stalk of grass. The assessor was suddenly conscious of what amounted to his orders to do his best to... what was the old-fashioned English expression? *Compromise* her.

Suppressing a sigh, he arose, for some reason stiffer in the joints than he was accustomed to being, thrust his hands in his pockets, and, leaving his sword behind on the blanket he'd occupied, ambled toward the girl as casually as he could manage. He'd known that they would find themselves together after this session. Somehow knowing didn't make it any better.

"Well, there you have it, a much more normal sort of procedure."

"No one beheaded," she glanced up briefly, "or impaled."

Not yet, he thought cynically as he reached to take her hand, surprised when she didn't flinch or withdraw. She was without doubt the most clumsy and unattractive young woman he'd ever known. Nothing he could say or do would change that. Despite hymns of altruism sung by the Soviet Americans, he was from a culture vastly more mature and knew that feeling sorry for the other party was no way to begin a relationship. It occurred to him that he'd felt many things during his brief acquaintance with Reille y Sanchez and Rosalind Nguyen, but he had never once felt sorry for either of them.

Letting go of her hand, he put his own at the small of her back above the waistband of her jumpsuit, guiding her across the glade to the blanket and sword he'd left behind. A dubious symbolism, he thought, groping for some inconsequential thing to say to fill the silent air about them. Words didn't come, and she was quiet, too. Soon enough they'd find themselves making love under the tree where his office and residence grew. Without saying it, both realized it was the same place where another woman had died at his hands. He thought of Rosalind and of a novelty postcard one of the Americans had told him about: "Having a wonderful time. Wish you were her."

By mutual consent, they remained standing, silence growing until it threatened to overwhelm them. "Let's climb a tree," Eichra Oren declared suddenly, trying to seize control of his existence again. "I've been meaning to take a closer look at what's happening with my house."

"Okay." There was relief and gratitude in her voice as she surveyed the giant before them for a foothold. It wasn't hard, even for him, encumbered by his sword and the accusing blanket. The spot they'd chosen was rough and furrowed, the barklike covering of the great green stalk and the way it spread to the roots almost forming stairs. Before they knew it, they'd reached the first branch and were looking down at a broad, flat, off-white shelf formed by the mushroomlike organism Eichra Oren had planted here. Various features of the house-to-be were already recognizable: partitions, deck railing, "built-in" furniture that looked closer to being half-melted than half-grown. At the back, nearest the trunk, sat the smooth-surfaced platform of a bed.

Eichra Oren tested the growth with a cautious foot, then stepped down solidly, taking Toya's hand—unnecessarily, in all likelihood—to help her down. She held on once she stood beside him and despite himself, he was gratified. He seemed—the cynical thought arose again—to be accomplishing the vile deed with marvelous dispatch. Mr. Thoggosh would be delighted. Of course Sam, who picked up slang from the Americans at a dismaying rate, would call it "shooting fish in a barrel." For his own part, everything he said to Toya or did with her made him feel like what they called a "heel." It would forever afterward, whenever he thought about it, but what were a few mortal consequences among friends, anyway?

What sickened him most was the way he'd derided the obsessive American concept of duty. Now it seemed the same consideration compelled him to make unfeeling love to this vulnerable young woman, and he could see with pitiful clarity how the prospect filled her with equal amounts of joy and terror. *Great Egg, she's a virgin!* He was about to hurt her, and himself, for no reason that struck him as particularly worthy, which meant that somehow he'd been corrupted by his contact with collectivism—and so had Mr. Thoggosh— and it was possible he'd never feel clean again.

Toya gasped. The muscles of Eichra Oren's arms were like wood where her shoulder blades lay across one as the other swept behind her knees to lift her off her feet and lay her down on the low platform. Fine hairs on the back of his hand glistened like gold wire as he reached to her throat for the toggle of her shipsuit zipper and pulled it as far below her waist as it would go.

In an instant she lay exposed to his eyes and hands as she had never been to any man, naked from the overprominent knobs of her collarbones to the first fair curls a handspan below her navel. A single syllable from her lips could make this rape or something else. Whatever she said, it wouldn't stop what was happening or change, very much, the way she felt about it.

She reached to lock her fingers into the thick bronze hair at the back of his neck as he pressed his mouth against a small, flat breast she was afraid might disappear altogether if she put her hand behind her own head. Even as she responded to his fingertips pressing their demands into her flesh, she was amazed at what she was doing. A warmth grew, somewhere between her knees and her waist, spreading upward and outward. Asked to describe herself, she'd have said tech sergeant, perhaps amateur paleontologist after that. "Woman" would never have been her thoughtless, automatic response.

He rolled aside and slipped a hand into her open coverall between her thighs, probing with a finger. A wave of shock and heat went through her, her blood sizzling in its wake as if carbonated. She felt limp, weak, about to slide off into sleep, but she was wide awake and focused in a way, and in a place within her mind, she'd never seen before and never knew existed.

All of her adult life, until just a little while ago, it had been her expectation that she would always be a virgin and would die, at whatever age, in the same unenviable state. She'd never dared dream of this, of finding this kind of happiness. (And she realized as, step-by-step, he claimed her body in his methodical, relentless way, that she *was* happy.) It wasn't a matter of having tried and failed. The fact was, fearing humiliation, she'd never tried at all. Such a thing had never consciously occurred to her. If it had, she wouldn't have had the courage. Nor was it that she'd been rejected by men. They hadn't ever noticed her enough to reject her.

Now, on this little island in space, deep within an alien forest, all that seemed to be changing. Toya never remembered how Eichra Oren got her arms out of her sleeves or the rest of the jumpsuit off her. All at once, he was above her and between her legs. She felt herself parting, felt pressure and a little pain, then wave after cool, white-hot wave of something wonderful and far beyond her power to describe.

Life, it appeared, was full of surprises.

"Well, that was certainly educational."

Sam approached Eichra Oren when he sat once again at the base of the canopy tree, lost in what he felt was a miserable substitute for thought. He was more than a little surprised, given the circumstances, that he'd been physically capable of doing what he'd just done. He was especially disturbed about where it had been accomplished, if "accomplished" was the word. Too many memories, all of them bad, lived here.

Having made love to Toya three times and sent her, dazed and happy, on her way back to the human camp, he'd immediately begun to feel guilty and to despise himself both for the deed and for the feeling it evoked.

"Wonderful," he told the dog, using the language of his people and the implant of the Elders. To an eavesdropper, the two would have appeared to be contemplating one another silently. "Did you watch the whole thing?"

"Would *I* violate the privacy of a fellow sapient?" Sam sat down beside his human friend, then stretched at length on the grass. He sighed. "Despite your late success, this hasn't been a very lucky assignment, has it, Boss?"

"I feel," Eichra Oren shook his head, "that I've been forced by circumstances to revert to a more primitive philosophical state here."

His friend gave the little bark that served him as a laugh. "Bullshit."

"Thanks." Eichra Oren paused, thinking. "You're right, though. It takes every scrap of honesty, integrity, character, and self-discipline I have not to blame somebody else—say the Americans—for what seems to be happening to me. What stings is that this is the very feeling my profession is supposed to help people overcome. Do away with."

Sam yawned, apparently unsympathetic, and rolled to scratch behind one ear. "Somebody told me that California's the only place in the universe where people feel guilty for feeling guilty."

The man ignored the dog. "More than that. I dread the moment when my assignment here is finished and I have to break things off and hurt her."

"And despite yourself, you're already mentally rehearsing the tragic scene?" The dog yawned again. "Give me a break, will you? All you're doing is smelling smoke and looking for a fire escape. You can't help it, Boss, it's a reflex. Individuals of my species chew their legs off when they're caught in a trap. In your case, I guess you'd have to chew off your—"

"What rankles most," the man interrupted, "is that the damage I'm inflicting on Toya and myself is all for nothing. The one I'm really angriest at, besides me, is Mr. Thoggosh. At him I'm very angry. And before you say a word, Sam, don't bother trying to talk me out of that minor satisfaction."

"Wouldn't dream of it. I know your opinion of the professional methods appropriate to this assignment, Boss. I share them. They don't include sucking face and parts south with a female you don't care for."

Eichra Oren grimaced. "They're corrupting you, too, Sam. That's about the most disgusting turn of phrase I've ever heard."

"For the most disgusting situation we've ever found ourselves in?"

"Well, it does seem Mr. Thoggosh requires me to play

the game, as the Americans put it, with one hand tied behind my back.'' He plucked a blade of grass, put it in his mouth, and thought of Rosalind and Toya, Toya and Rosalind. ''Sam, I can't protect the Elders' precious secrets unless I know what those secrets are. On more than one occasion, I've all but begged that old bag of ink to be more open with me. He seems to regard this whole matter as something personal, something reserved exclusively to the Elders, something they apparently believe doesn't involve any other species.''

Sam looked up. ''Boss, have you ever suspected that this assignment is just a convenient way to keep you out of Mr. Thoggosh's figurative hair?''

''More than once,'' the man conceded. ''On other occasions, I suspect that something even more sinister might be happening. . . .''

Sam grinned, ''You show me your paranoia, I'll show you mine.''

''Well''—he spat out a bit of leaf and frowned—''remember that we made as detailed a study of this culture as time permitted. And in the course of that study, we ran across all sorts of bizarre ideas either abandoned long ago by the Elders or never invented by them in the first place. Among them, you'll recall, was this infantile tendency, present in most primitive cultures, which these particular humans don't seem able to outgrow. They believe things without sufficient evidence—often in the face of proof to the contrary—simply because they *want* to believe them.''

The dog responded sourly, ''We're talking Yahweh and Company here?''

Eichra Oren nodded. ''That infantile tendency's most conspicuous result is the survival and proliferation of religions long past the period when, in any other culture, they ought to have begun to wither and die.''

Sam shook his head, a very human gesture. ''It looks to me, Boss, like the situation's worse than that, a matter of permanent, deadly fixation at the most primitive stage of cultural development.''

''I don't think we contradict one another,'' the man told him. ''Look, with these people, mysticism forms, along with altruism and collectivism, a tight, mutually supportive, impenetrable network of roots which bind the human mind and make further progress impossible.''

''And what you're hoping—'' Sam's tone fell to an uncharacteristically serious level. ''Pardon the, uh, overpertinent comment, Boss, but I can't help observing your confusion and unhappiness. You only hope the condition isn't as contagious as you think it might be.''

Eichra Oren closed his eyes, breathed in deeply, and exhaled, relieved to hear the words. ''Something like that, yes.''

''It ain't likely,'' the dog argued. ''One thing separating you from your fellow apes here is the history of your people with respect to mysticism. How many times have I heard your mother say that their most popular religion was pretty feeble and uncomplicated to begin with, and that it was already feeling the discouraging effects of early scientific progress by the time the Continent was Lost?''

''Yes, my fellow apes, as you charmingly put it, are comparing what they call 'Antarctica' with England in its eighteenth century, when this culture should have started shedding its religions. I don't know what went wrong. For my people, the polar reversal and climatic disaster finished off anybody's faith in benevolent deities. And among those refugees who were 'collected,' exposure to the rational philosophy of the Elders did the rest.''

Sam snorted, ''Whereas it would have made these jerks *more* religious. So what's the point, if you don't mind me asking—or even if you do.''

''Nothing I can put a finger on, just the general feel of a bad situation. I'm beginning to suspect Mr. Thoggosh, and you'll appreciate how it dismays me, especially since it's none of my business, of something like religious motivations. In every respect, Sam, this disquieting affair smells of the irrational—and that from someone with a nose a million times less sensitive than yours, my canine friend.'' He shook his head. ''It's uncharacteristic of the Elders in general and of Mr. Thoggosh in particular.''

''Religious motivations?'' The dog looked him in the eye. ''I'd say that rancid old mollusc's behavior is uncharacteristic of the normal relationship between himself and you, and that's what really worries you.''

Eichra Oren stood up. ''One way or another, Sam, I've come to a decision. I'm going to ferret out the Elders' secret on my own. With respect to what Mr. Thoggosh wants, that will put me closer, faster, to anyone else trying to do the same. Also, and this is no small consideration, it might satisfy my professional and personal curiosity.''

Sam got to his feet as well and wagged his tail. ''Make that 'on *our* own,' Boss, and you've got a deal!''

XIII
Four-footed Legwork

''Yes, Nannel Rab, I know, I know.''

Having decided, Eichra Oren didn't wait. Before another hour had gone by, Sam was keeping an appointment—rather, he was spending more time than he cared to cooling his nonexistent heels as the appointee attended to other chores. Eichra Oren was off on another part of the asteroid.

''Yes, yes, Nannel Rab, I know.''

At the moment, Aelbraugh Pritsch was speaking with Mr. Thoggosh's chief engineer, his words spoken into empty air while his thoughts traveled halfway around the little world via implant. He and Sam were in a building that served the feathered being as office and quarters, a rambling structure that never seemed the same whenever Sam visited Mr. Thoggosh's assistant. The plan was open, without floors or partitions. It was a multistory maze of crisscrossing stairways, perches, and swings unique to the warm-blooded avian dinosauroid species. Aelbraugh Pritsch delighted in rearranging it every chance he got, although it confused his nonavian, nondinosauroid associates.

"I know it isn't working. I merely observed that it meets the standards originally specified. I don't see how a debt assessment would help. We're here, the manufacturer's back home. We must make do with what we have."

Sam dreaded continuing the conversation. Eichra Oren's 'disrespectful attitude' and 'disorderly methodology' upset Aelbraugh Pritsch, a capable individual in his own fussy way, although it pained Sam to admit it. He was neither by personality nor inborn nature a happy soul. Sam thought he knew why, although he'd never been able to persuade Eichra Oren. The species had descended from forms which, over the course of evolution, had lost the ability to fly. Flying was a biologically expensive strategy. Flying creatures often found easier ways of staying alive: ostriches had sacrificed wings for size and running speed; penguins followed the way of the seal. Giving up flight had freed dinosauroid brains, already well developed for the three-dimensional task of flying, to do other things. Mostly, it appeared to Sam, worrying.

"Yes, I'll ask about ion implantation. If it's within my power..."

In many respects, too, beings like Aelbraugh Pritsch remained creatures of the flock. In their world they were used to hierarchy and predictability. Unlike humans (and dogs) they'd never felt at ease as Appropriated Persons, although they'd been collected in greater numbers than any other species due to their habit of staying in large groups.

The Elders' laissez-faire informality, a result of their sophisticated history, went against the avians' bent as badly as Eichra Oren's personality which, to a degree, reflected that history.

"The Americans? Why, you're right, Nannel Rab. Their ships do show evidence of ion hardening. If in need of a dugout canoe, ask a savage. But you'll have to do your own asking. My time is occupied."

It didn't help that Aelbraugh Pritsch was aware of all this, or that by avian standards he was a loner bordering on the psychotic. Avians tended to strike others as neurotic anyway. They, in turn, had long ago given up pointing to the difficulties others experienced adjusting to life with the nautiloids. By all rights, he ought to have gotten along with the newly arrived humans, professed altruists and collectivists that they were, but by nature they were no more creatures of the flock than he was an individualist. Sam had noticed he could hardly stand to be around them.

"Where were we?" Aelbraugh Pritsch had finished with the engineer. "Doesn't Eichra Oren realize the risk he incurs? He's supposed to protect the Elders' privacy. Yet someone—anyone—staying one step behind him in the course of his investigation would benefit from whatever he discovers."

"He wondered whether you'd been let in on the Proprietor's secret."

"I certainly haven't," came the answer, "nor, considering the terrible responsibility, do I wish to be. I've too much responsibility of my own."

"Aren't you curious," Sam asked, "about why you came to 5023 Eris?"

"If I were, I wouldn't be doing my job, would I?" *So there*, Sam mentally completed the thought. "Need I add that those associated with the Elders are hardly monolithic in their views? They begin with the intransigence natural to them and then, thanks to the Elders, add half a billion years of disharmony to that. Humans like Eichra Oren are unruly to the last cell of their bodies, incapable of acting as an unprotesting unit. From their arrival, it puzzled me how Americans ever talked themselves into socialism. Generations have passed, still they spend each waking minute writhing in the discomfort of it, imposing it by force on one another. For all they've achieved, they might as well be pachyderms flapping their ears and trying to fly.''

Sam had seen an animated movie on that subject, but didn't mention it. ''You complain that they're *trying* to be monolithic?''

''I complain that they act against their nature. I live among natural individualists and to an extent, because I'm sapient, have become one myself. Yet for my species, it isn't necessary to adopt an ideology; we naturally sort ourselves into a 'pecking hierarchy' and obey orders. To us it feels as if that's what we've chosen freely. Before the advent of the Elders, we had to *invent* a semblance of individualism in order to advance. In that respect, I sympathize with these Marxists. Collectivism can't be any more comfortable for them than its opposite is to my people.''

''A difference being,'' Sam offered, ''that collectivism fails to benefit them the way individualism did your people. But we've digressed.''

''We have. I understand that any preference on my part that others be more like me is doomed. That's the danger I foresee in this scheme of Eichra Oren's. Like individuals everywhere, some among our party have looser tongues than others. Others disagree with the necessity of keeping under cover.''

''Or the dignity,'' Sam interposed.

''Or the dignity. Have it your own way.''

''I try to,'' the dog replied absently. A light had begun flashing in his mind at Aelbraugh Pritsch's last words, but he couldn't pin it down.

Tongues, loose or otherwise, had nothing to do with the Elders themselves, who spoke by radio produced by the same sort of cells that make some eels electric. Despite the fact that it was their expedition, few had come here besides Mr. Thoggosh and the late Semlochcolresh. With Pulaski in tow, Eichra Oren made short work of interviewing half a dozen of them. Now the assessor was traveling all over the asteroid in search of answers.

At the moment they sat with a third individual on packing crates in a large tent overlooking one of the drilling sites that seemed to be the reason for the colony's existence, while a fourth, incapable of sitting, stood nearby. All about were scattered reminders—folded cots, stretchers, stacks of bandages, metal and plastic implements—of an emergency safely past.

"Dear me, yes," Dlee Raftan Saon told them. The surgeon resembled a giant praying mantis. "When a piece of machinery that size comes apart at a hundred fifty thousand gigavolts, there are bound to be injuries no matter how hardy the species involved." He turned his head to look at Nannel Rab, a spider nine feet tall, covered in black and red-orange fur. Toya found the engineer beautiful and repelling at the same time, although her beauty was marred just now by surgical dressings over a large area of her great abdomen. "I'm grateful no one was killed, thank Nannel Rab's quick thinking. She heard the plasma drill begin to fail and ordered evacuation. Those I treated had dorsal shrapnel wounds, including Nannel Rab herself."

Nannel Rab waved a modest palp. "You are too kind, Dlee Raftan Saon. I merely performed as any rational being—"

"Perhaps, my dear," the insect-being replied before the giant spider could finish, "but there are too few rational beings in the universe."

"Yes," Toya put in impatiently, "but you haven't told us what they were drilling *for*, Dlee Raftan Saon."

He emitted wheezing noises she'd learned to interpret as a chuckle. "You noticed. That's because I haven't the faintest idea."

Eichra Oren shook his head. "And you aren't curious?"

"I'm consumed with curiosity. I had hoped, somewhat unethically, to learn something from my patients under anesthesia. You'd be surprised what we hear that way. But we made do with topicals, so I'll have to wait until another time—may fortune forfend." He wheezed again.

"But you're a partner in this enterprise, aren't you?" Toya protested.

"You don't think I'd come here for professional fees?"

"Then how can you not—"

"Rather than promise not to divulge something I might find interesting to talk about, I refused Mr. Thoggosh's explanation and trusted his judgment. Isn't it more fun" —he lowered his voice and wheezed—"guessing?"

"Some fun!"

Eichra Oren grinned. "What have you guessed so far?"

"It's my impression," Dlee Raftan Saon scratched at a mouth part, "that it concerns development of sophisticated technology, involving unconventional application of certain philosophical principles."

The assessor blinked. "That's a hell of a guess, even if it's wrong."

"I'm a good guesser—that's what diagnostics is about, after all."

"In that case," Nannel Rab put in, "I had better obtain a second medical opinion. The most charitable speculation is that this mission is nothing more than an archaeological expedition."

Eichra Oren raised an eyebrow. "And the least charitable?"

"We look for treasure."

The physician gave an almost human shrug. "Well, some of it Mr. Thoggosh told me in the first place to get me interested. As to the rest, I keep my eyes open. I haven't any choice; unlike yours, they have no lids!" He was still wheezing to himself as they left in search of their next subject.

Toya couldn't decide what Voozh Preeno was.

The creature was the result of impressive evolutionary

divergence. He, she, or it (she hadn't learned much about this assistant logistics specialist) might be distantly related to anemones, urchins, even the starfish at Eichra Oren's session. On the other hand, Voozh Preeno might descend from organisms as diverse as fan corals, arachnids, even intelligent plants—its overall color was a pale green—like Llessure Knarrfic. Sam would say it was an extroverted hairball a meter in diameter. Observation revealed dozens of fibrous tentacles rising from an unseen center, branching into dozens of smaller appendages which branched into dozens more. The finest tendrils at the ends of all that branching were specialized. What kept Voozh Preeno from looking like a furry beachball was the fact that, as it moved, when it ''walked'' or ''handed'' her the drink she accepted for the sake of observing it, it appeared to split, revealing a coarser inner structure. She still wasn't sure whether there was any central body or it consisted entirely of limbs.

''Truth is a valuable commodity,'' it informed Eichra Oren, ''which we do not automatically owe anyone. I am, moreover, honor-bound to withhold it. That is more than you would learn did I offer you an engaging falsehood.''

''Well put, Voozh Preeno,'' a fourth individual declared. ''With eight legs, you might have been a Minister of the Royal Web.''

Like Nannel Rab, Nek Nam'l Las was a spider of daunting proportions—arachnids appeared to be highly successful across time, and these two didn't represent the only species of sapient spiders Toya had heard of—but that was where the resemblance ceased. The engineer was black and red. Nek Nam'l Las was blue-black from palp to spinneret. Nannel Rab was descended from solitary hunters. Nek Nam'l Las's ancestors had been gregarious web-spinners.

''You flatter me, Your Highness, but I enjoy it.''

Eichra Oren stood. He'd been sitting on the floor. ''We thank you for that much, Voozh Preeno. Ready, Toya?''

'' 'Your Highness'?'' Toya was confused. Why was Eichra

Oren giving up so easily? "I thought your society didn't have any government."

The sleek black form, a meter taller than the girl, turned on its legs to focus several eyes on her. "We haven't, little warm one. Our noblesse oblige is *not* to rule so that anarchy is free to reign without a vacuum begging to be filled. Thus it has been for generations among my kind on our world and among those of us caught in the Elders' web of power and transported to theirs."

"The princess is the highest of her line among the Appropriated Persons," Voozh Preeno explained.

Toya shook her head. "And a humble logistics officer at the same time?"

The spider raised a foreleg. "Those who will not endure *social* equality condemn themselves to suffer the *political* variety in its place."

Toya set down her glass, which had been filled with ordinary tomato juice—she hoped. These quarters seemed ordinary, too, their only odd feature a vat of oily fluid in place of the usual sleeping platform. She played with the idea that the Elders had accidentally collected at least one extraterrestrial in all that sampling fifteen thousand years ago.

They were back at the Elders' Settlement to question beings from a list Eichra Oren had made, having spoken with dozens more across the asteroid. The results weren't different, she suspected, from those obtained on Earth by a conventional detective. This wasn't the first refusal they'd elicited, along with a mixture of unrelated facts, unsupported theories, and outright lies. Some species felt that it was the polite alternative. Out of this mixture, the stubborn investigator was trying to sift, one microscopic hint at a time, something resembling the truth. At least he'd been stubborn until now.

She got to her feet. "Thank you, Voozh Preeno. Sometime I'd like to speak with you about your people. I'm interested in evolution."

"And you wonder what I am, Sergeant Pulaski?"

"Toya. Yes, I hope you don't mind."

Voozh Preeno laughed. Toya didn't know where its voice came from, but it sounded human. "Other sapients often have trouble placing us. Your interest is generally shared in the culture the Elders have helped us create. It would be strange if this were not the case."

She nodded. "I suppose it would."

"To answer your question: you are distantly related to chordates, like sharks. Well, through an indirect process which makes us a younger species than the Elders, my people are related to sponges. Before you ask your next question, I am both male and female, although I am gratified to say we mate with others of our species rather than ourselves. That is biologically unproductive and considered a perversion."

Toya nodded gravely and thanked Voozh Preeno for explaining.

"But stay, mammals." Nek Nam'l Las wheeled until she stood between them and the door. Toya felt a chill run down her spine. "I relish the odor of your blood. And you have not yet asked for my opinion."

Eichra Oren reached up to stroke the furry palp of the giant towering over him and another chill coursed through Toya's body. "I thought it more respectful, Princess, to wait until you offered."

Nek Nam'l Las turned to the girl. "The expression among your kind is 'in a pig's valise,' is it not? Eichra Oren, you have never been respectful of anyone. But I am subject to no promise of secrecy and have heard it said that Mr. Thoggosh seeks a faster-than-light technology called the 'Virtual Drive.' Was that not worth the risk of being eaten alive?"

"Your Highness"—he touched her again—"I'll repay you with my firstborn child the second Thursday of next week. You'll find it a succulent tidbit for your web."

"Not if half as acerbic as yourself. Farewell, delicious friend, and you, as well, Toya Pulaski."

Her hand shaking, Toya reached up to stroke the coarse fur of the creature's face, then hurried out the door. In the corridor, Eichra Oren turned. "You survived that rather well. What are you trying not to laugh about?"

Toya giggled. "Perversion. I don't know about going blind, but Voozh Preeno seems to have grown a lot of hair on its palms."

"And," he grinned back at her, "everywhere else."

She shook her head. "I like your cannibal princess. Where to next?"

"The infirmary," he told her, "and Remaulthiek."

Another thing Toya couldn't figure out was why Eichra Oren chose certain individuals to question. The creature whom Americans had first labeled a "walking quilt" dispensed refreshments at the infirmary and was also a partner in Mr. Thoggosh's enterprise. Why Eichra Oren thought she'd violate the contract to tell him of the mission here, Toya couldn't guess. They found her, another of the chordates Voozh Preeno had mentioned (more closely resembling a ray than a shark), sitting beside her cart, having a meal on a lawn before the infirmary.

"Greetings, Remaulthiek, how do you do?"

"I do not return your greeting, but keep it for my collection. By eating, Eichra Oren, as you see now, and by getting enough sleep."

The human shook his head. "I'm sorry, I didn't mean 'how is it that you exist.' I meant to inquire as to your state of being."

Remaulthiek, glistening within the covering that kept her gills moist, stretched to the cart for another sandwich. "It continues," she told him, "as it has for some time now. This is one of the new ones?"

"Toya Pulaski. We've come to ask you questions, if we may."

"There are better answerers than I. What do you wish to ask?"

"I want to know why the Elders came to 5023 Eris. What—"

"I interrupt," Remaulthiek told him, "saving you much time and further effort. We are here because we seek after the gods."

With a disappointed expression, Eichra Oren opened his mouth, but was interrupted again. "Gods?" Toya asked.

"Those who no longer manifest themselves upon this plane of existence," came the reply. "Was not this made clear to you?"

The girl sat down beside the creature. "It's supposed to be a secret. Didn't Mr. Thoggosh swear you to secrecy when you signed his agreement?"

"My kind make no agreement, human person, but do as we say and deny not reality. This is not so with other species. We respect the ways of others."

"I see." Eichra Oren's words followed a long silence while the creature contemplated her sandwich. "What happened to these gods, Remaulthiek?"

"They departed long ago. Know you nothing of unnatural history?"

"It's my place to seek the truth. How long ago did they depart?"

"Close upon the ninth order. We partners seek to follow them."

XIV
Two-legged Footwork

As the asteroid rotated into night and the canopy darkened overhead, Sam was returning to the temporary quarters he shared with Eichra Oren, thinking about his unproductive interview with Aelbraugh Pritsch and of one or two similar conversations that had followed it.

Tl*m*nch*l, the chief of security, was one of the sapient crustaceans the Soviet Americans called "giant bugs with guns." Asked what he knew of the nautiloids' purpose on 5023 Eris, Tl*m*nch*l had expressed his belief that, after a hiatus lasting fifteen thousand years, the Elders were again seeking other alternate-world beings. On the other hand Clym Pucras, the machine-tool designer Eichra Oren had heard in a professional capacity, argued that if the mission were seeking anything, it was traces of a vanished race of sapients older than the Elders, now extinct in all known versions of the System. Neither being had offered much in the way of evidence to support his position.

At the moment, Sam was wondering whether Eichra Oren had given him this assignment to keep him out from underfoot regarding Toya. They would soon leave this impersonal apartment, he thought, but not a moment too soon. He wondered whether Eichra Oren would be coming home tonight. He was too proud, or he wasn't sure what, to contact the man and ask. When not actively assisting his companion, he often succumbed to periods of lonely meditation. It appeared he might have a night of it ahead of him to look forward to.

"Hello, Sam."

Someone was waiting at the door. "Hello, Dr. Nguyen. Eichra Oren isn't here right now and I don't know when he'll be back." Sam liked her. She was small and soft and golden brown. Despite a lingering hint of disinfectant perceptible only to his canine senses, she always smelled good. He waited for her reply before going inside.

"That's all right, Sam. It's you I wanted to see, anyway. I wish you'd call me Rosalind. May I come in, please?"

"Follow me." He was surprised and pleased. Scutigera's wry observation was correct to an extent. He preferred the conversation and company of human females to that of his own kind, although it had never gone further than that, despite the centipede's innuendo. "Can I fix you something to drink?"

She was looking around, but it didn't take long because there wasn't much to see. "In a little while, perhaps. There's something I'd like to ask you about first, if you don't mind."

Another thing Sam liked about her was that she didn't ask, as many of her fellow humans had already, how he could accomplish something like fixing her a drink when he didn't have any hands. "I will if I can. Please find a chair." He hopped onto a corner of the bed, lay down on his belly, and crossed one paw over the other. "What's all this about—Rosalind?"

Across the little room she smiled, but her tone was grim and there was no relaxation in her posture. "Sam, there's a rumor going around about Sergeant Pulaski, that she's been given a special assignment by the KGB. You probably remember that Estrellita—Major Reille y Sanchez—was the last one to be given such an assignment. You're aware what happened to her."

He nodded. "You're worried that the same thing might happen to Toya?"

She bit her lip and nodded. "There's no end to the surprises on this asteroid. Startling, mind-altering discoveries. Why most of them should center on the only human among the nautiloids is more than I can—"

"You're afraid that, like her predecessor, Toya may make the *wrong* discoveries about Eichra Oren? That isn't what killed Estrellita, although I must admit that the private life and personal statistics of a *p'Nan* debt assessor, of any human being if you ask me—no offense—are more bizarre the more you learn about them. Somehow I feel that isn't what you're getting at."

"It could be." She shook her head, contradicting herself. "Most of his friends and clients are such alien creatures. Like that giant centipede—"

"I was just thinking of Scutigera. Don't forget Oasam the Wonderdog."

She went on as if she hadn't heard him, locking her fingers together and staring at the floor. "On the other hand, my life among sapients of only one species must seem narrow and dull to him. Until I began meeting his friends, this hadn't occurred to me," she concluded glumly. "And no, I'm not forgetting Sam the Wonderdog. It's icing on the cake that his best friend and assistant happens to be a cybernetically augmented sapient canine."

"Best friend and assistant. Watson to his Holmes, eh what? Let me tell you something about that—although I thought this was about Toya—but first I'd better fix you that drink I promised. What'll you have?"

"Nothing alcoholic, thanks," she smiled. "This visit is professional, technically, and I'm on call."

"Nothing alcoholic coming up!" He nodded at a wall panel which melted away to reveal a shelf of glasses beneath a row of dispensers. A glass slid from one nozzle to another, filling itself with a brown, foamy liquid. The niche was closer to Rosalind than Sam. She rose and took the glass before the wall went solid and sat down again.

She drank, then looked up. "Why this is—Sam, the formula for this is supposed to be a trade secret. How—"

"Another advantage," he grinned, "of being able to crack any code. I was about to tell you that my kind were intended by the Elders as nothing more than remote-controlled conveniences. I'm supposed to serve Eichra Oren the same way Mr. Thoggosh's detachable limb serves him. But somewhere, the nautiloids' biological engineers made a mistake. I'm much more than that—all of my kind are—both to myself and my 'master.'"

"I see that." She took another sip. "What do you mean, specifically?"

Sam gave it thought. "Well, I learned recently from you Americans about guide dogs for the blind."

Rosalind nodded. "A better analogy than you know, Sam." She hesitated, then: "You may have to be Eichra Oren's 'thinking-brain dog' for a while. He seems to be having trouble in that department himself lately."

"Bringing us to the purpose of this conversation?" he chuckled. "I can't say I haven't been worried about him, although if I were truly man's best friend—I'll settle for being his partner. It isn't always easy. In fact, I often find myself wondering . . ."

There was a long, empty silence.

"Wondering what?" Rosalind asked.

"Suppose the Elders had kept searching fifteen thousand years ago, through the infinite worlds of probability. Mightn't they have found a reality in which dogs grew hands and walked erect and invented technology so they'd have more time to spend wallowing in self-doubt? You know, all the things that make you human?"

She laughed openly and honestly. He liked the sound of it. "Sam, this is about you, isn't it? You must know that you're liked simply for yourself. That's especially true of us Americans who don't know anything about any role you're supposed to play in nautiloid society. It doesn't matter to me anyway, and I don't think any of us see you as a mere appendage, to Eichra Oren or anybody else. Besides, in that other universe you're talking about, you might not even recognize the evolutionary result as a dog. They might not recognize you. To those canine somethings somewhere, you'd be like a . . .''

"Like a gorilla to your people? Somehow that fails to comfort me."

She raised her eyebrows. "Is that what I was supposed to do? I thought I came to ask you questions. Seriously, I'm curious about all sorts of things. For example, what's it like to be tied in permanently to a sort of mental-computer bulletin-board system?''

He had to think for a moment before he realized what she was getting at. "You mean the implant network?"

"Yes, to me it's a real wonder, given that item of technology, that individualism has survived at all among the nautiloids. I'd have expected it to be swept away by all their brain-penetrating machinery.''

"Well, it's another analogy to something the elders were born with. They had several hundred million years to get used to it. The Elder who invented what you'd call the Faraday cage—and mental privacy—is revered as the greatest . . . nautiloiditarian . . . who ever lived. Even if what you say about individualism is true, there was no one with the power to do the sweeping. It wouldn't be the same on your world, would it?''

"There we agree. The fact is, nothing is the same here. Just as an example, strangest of the strange: Sam, that burden which has rested heaviest on human shoulders throughout all recorded and inferred history has no influence whatever on you or Eichra Oren or any of your associates.''

He cocked his head. "Now you've lost me."

"I know." She grinned and he knew she'd been struck all over again by the contrast between the conversation and the kind of being she was having it with. "Whatever else we agree on, it makes for a fundamental difference between us. We might as well be different species, people like Eichra

Oren and myself. It's like a chronic debtor trying to imagine the world from the viewpoint of someone who has never had to worry about money.''

"It's true we're a wealthy culture, but—"

She shook her head vehemently. "I'm not talking about wealth—or I am, but not about money. In my experience, my people's experience, men and women are confronted from their first adult thought, maybe even their first waking moment, with the inevitable prospect of aging and death. I often heard my father lament that, just as he was beginning to acquire some skill at living his life, it was beginning to end. As it happened, he died prematurely, even for someone of his time and place, at the age of fifty-nine.''

"I'm sorry.'' Sam didn't know what else to say.

She looked down at her hands. "So was he. He hated it. No amount of talk about what's normal ever made him hate it less. I feel the same way. It may be natural, but it doesn't feel *right*. I think that's why I became a doctor. Nevertheless, I've always lived with the fact that I, too, will grow old, get wrinkled, become feeble, and eventually die.'' She looked up at him. "Species associated with the nautiloids, however, everybody in the category of 'Appropriated Persons,' enjoy extraordinarily long lives, don't they?''

Sam nodded. "By your standards. It was part of the Great Restitution the Elders made for having removed them from their native environments.''

"That much I know. There were other benefits: cerebrocortical implants, useful companions like yourself, full participation in nautiloid society, whatever that means. Somehow, knowing Mr. Thoggosh, I doubt it has anything to do with voting. I'm certain it has nothing to do with taxes. But—'' Her expression changed. Suddenly she was a small child wanting answers. "How *long* do they live, Sam? Until now, I haven't been able to find out.''

"Probably because nobody knows.''

She frowned, puzzled. "How can that be?''

"Well . . .'' Weary of the position he was in, Sam slid

onto the floor, stretched, then crossed the room. To Rosalind's left was a small table and beside that, another chair. He hopped onto it and sat. She turned to face him, both hands on the left arm of her chair. "The Antarctican disaster occurred fifteen thousand years ago, when the Earth's magnetic poles shifted naturally, as they do from time to time, disrupting the planet's climate. A civilization was buried beneath a fall of permanent snow. Soon that snow became two miles of glacial ice which still cover the continent in our time."

She was impatient. "I've heard this. What does it have to do with—"

"I'm getting to it, Doctor. Antarctican culture was cut off almost at the initial moment of its greatest achievements—"

She sat back, relaxing for the first time since she'd entered the room. "I've been told it was about where England was at the time of Napoleon."

"Seems about right," Sam agreed. "They had fair maps, good navigation, very good ships for all that they were wood built and wind powered. When the climate changed, some Antarcticans took to these sophisticated sailboats and escaped, to the place you call India. But a shipload was 'collected' by the Elders during one of their remote surveys." He paused, trying to think of how to phrase the next idea. "That happened fifteen millennia ago, long before the present civilization on Earth. But there are a few human beings still alive—in the Elders' universe—who personally remember it."

Rosalind sat up and stared at him. *"What?"*

"Eneri Relda, Eichra Oren's mother, for one, sort of a living legend. She was a girl of seventeen or eighteen at the time, and still looks about that age."

Rosalind sat back again, shut her eyes, and marveled, "You're telling me she's older than the sequoias, older than the bristlecones . . ."

"That's what I'm telling you. She's older than the pyramids, the tablets of Sumeria, and the legend of Gilgamesh. She's three times as old as the entire length of recorded human history—which, I suspect, says more about recorded human history than it does about Eneri Relda.''

Rosalind was visibly stunned, but Sam knew she had the advantage of the best general scientific education her rather narrow and impoverished culture was capable of providing. He made some comment to that effect. Until now, she answered, she'd concentrated mostly on fields related to space travel—problems of free-fall, acceleration, decompression, and radiation.

''Still, I have enough general biology to know that there's no reason why the relatively small handful of degenerative diseases we collectively refer to as 'aging' should forever remain incurable. Every one has been arrested or slowed in lab animals.'' She shrugged. ''Having an imagination better than my education, I confess that I believe it, in part, simply because I want to.''

''As Eichra Oren might have predicted,'' Sam sighed. Life, apparently, had never been so miserable for Rosalind that she was unwilling to extend it. Maybe there was hope for these people, after all.

Rosalind blinked at him. ''How's that?''

''I was just thinking out loud.''

''Then so will I. Sam, I wonder what living one hundred fifty centuries feels like. Does time continue to pass more quickly as you grow older? Do the decades seem to flee like weeks for someone fifteen thousand years old? Are the centuries beginning to seem like nothing more than years to Eneri Relda?''

''It isn't the kind of thing one asks, Rosalind. Maybe time reaches some sort of cruising speed and levels off, I don't know. I can tell you that Eneri Relda is unusual in another respect—it's why I brought her up in the first place. The average human living among the Elders has an indefinite theoretical lifespan. But in practical terms, that means a considerably shorter life expectancy than hers, although it hasn't anything to do with aging or disease, but with statistics.''

"Oh?"

"Sure. People at home run the usual gamut from adventurers and athletes to what you call 'couch potatoes.' They have the technology to eradicate biological maladies. Even relatively serious injuries can be dealt with by nautiloid science. But sooner or later almost everyone among the Elders, including the Elders themselves, dies violently, simply because unpredictable catastrophes of one kind or another are the only thing left to die *from*."

Rosalind shuddered and wrapped her arms about herself. "What a prospect to look forward to. I wonder how they live with it."

"You should ask," Sam grinned, "whether the inevitable prospect of violent death is too much to pay for prolonged life."

She blinked. "I find that easy to answer, Sam. If that's the price, it's cheap. How long could I expect to live, statistically?"

He reached up to scratch an ear. "A thousand years, give or take."

"A thousand years." She set her mouth. "And Eichra Oren?"

"I thought you'd never ask. He's a youngster, Rosalind. On his last birthday, as I recall, he was a mere five hundred forty-two years old."

XV
The Predecessors

"Hang on, General! These things are supposed to compensate for g's but—*whoops!*"

Toya slid against the tense form of Gutierrez as the electrostat they occupied banked suddenly to avoid one of the great canopy plants. The machine had no seatbelts—no seats at all, for that matter—no visible controls, and its smooth, sloping interior threatened to spill them out at any moment, dashing them against a tree or into the cratered ground at what the general estimated, between gasps, was five hundred klicks per hour.

"That was *too damn close!*" Gutierrez squeezed his eyes shut and shuddered, suffering the pangs of an experienced combat pilot with someone else—in this instance, an invisible, electronic someone else—at the controls. What made it worse was that they didn't know where they were going. They'd been summoned by Eichra Oren only minutes ago when the unpiloted and unannounced aerocraft had settled in the middle of camp and paged Toya through some sort of public address system. When she answered, the Antarctican had insisted that she bring Gutierrez along.

"Y-yes, sir!" Although she was unaware of it, Toya wasn't the first to observe that there was no end to the surprises 5023 Eris could hand them. She'd been shocked already by the discovery that Mr. Thoggosh had left even Eichra Oren in the dark regarding his activities on the asteroid. She was convinced the Antarctican was being open with her about this ridiculous situation and had never been told the facts. It meant that the assignment Gutierrez and the KGB had given her was meaningless.

On the other hand, she didn't want to give up her newfound relationship and hoped perhaps she could get the answers her superiors demanded in another manner. Working together, with Sam's help, she and Eichra Oren had begun questioning other sapients, beings hired to work toward some goal that none of them, apparently, knew much about. The only reason they were here, aside from excellent pay and possible adventure, was a reputation Mr. Thoggosh had earned for historic undertakings that nearly always turned out profitable. Like Eichra Oren, most had been left out by their employer. A few others, partners like Scutigera, had been sworn to secrecy.

Eichra Oren reasoned, however, that each might possess a tiny piece of the puzzle, by virtue of various tasks and responsibilities he, she, or it was assigned. He was determined to gather all of this "need-to-know" information and try to assemble it. So far, laborious questioning had only given the would-be detective a few leads—and probably a lot of disinformation.

"Look out!" Toya watched Gutierrez watching another giant tree whirl past at dizzying velocity and a stomach-wrenching angle. Before they'd quite gotten used to the little craft—this was the first such trip for the general and Toya's previous rides had been rather more sedate—it slowed to a hover, lowering them gently to the ground.

They found themselves in a steep-walled canyon choked with vegetation. At the bottom a wide space had been cleared—the crisply singed tops of many larger plants hinted that something like a laser had been used—and promptly filled again with the same heavy equipment and bustling personnel Toya had seen at other drilling sites.

"Well, that was enough exhilaration for the next twenty years or so." Gutierrez stood up and tested his legs, which seemed to be less wobbly than he'd expected. Sweat trickled from his hair, down the side of his neck, into his uniform collar. Even through the canopy, the sun seemed brighter, hotter, and the atmosphere noticeably thicker in the depths of the canyon. "Given that long—and a good enough supply of tranquilizers—I might even get used to it. Now that we're here, Sergeant, where do you suppose 'here' is?"

"No-Name Gulch, according to Sam, here," a familiar human voice behind them answered the general's rhetorical question. "Mr. Thoggosh thinks it may be an impact fissure. Or his geologists do. It's the largest—and deepest—physical feature on 5023 Eris."

They turned. Eichra Oren and Sam were approaching the aerocraft, the former casually, with his hands in his pockets, the latter with bright eyes and his tongue hanging out. Toya and Gutierrez clambered through a section of the hull that swung out of the way.

"Somehow," the general replied, "I have a nagging suspicion that scientific sightseeing wasn't why you called us out here in such a hurry."

Eichra Oren grinned. "Well, General, in a way you could say it's scientific sightseeing. We came in almost as much haste as you did, summoned in almost the same way by Dlee Raftan Saon." The man hooked a thumb over his shoulder. "He's waiting for us now, at the field infirmary."

Together, the four walked toward the walled tent Toya had seen set up a day earlier, half a world away. This time there was no visible emergency. Inside, the physician was puttering with a bank of instruments arrayed atop a folding table. Hunched over his equipment, more than ever he reminded her of a praying mantis. Odd clumps of short, stiff bristles protruded from his joints which were like those of a crab or lobster. Perhaps oddest of all, he wore a long white cotton four-armed laboratory jacket.

She recognized from her AeroSpace Force basic training days the oddly pleasant and familiar smell of tautly stretched and sun-warmed canvas. The floor was canvas, too, lumpy and uneven under foot. It seemed cooler and dimmer within the tent, although it brightened now and then as the doorflap blew open and shut in an impressive breeze funneling down the canyon.

"Here you are!" he exclaimed without looking up. "General, Sergeant, I thought you might be as interested to see this as our friends, here."

His head turned on his armored shoulders. He indicated Sam and Eichra Oren, then the electronics on the table before him. "What you see here, my friends, is a sort of instant antique I ordered constructed this morning, a little as if you, sir, were to ask your Corporal Owen to build you a crystal radio receiver. It's a giant analog to the cybernetic implants most of us wear snuggled against whatever we happen to use for brains, intended for use by people like yourselves who are bereft of cortical implants.''

Toya could see that it looked like the sort of tabletop computer one might still find in an office at home. Those aboard the shuttles looked entirely different. The thing plugged into a small, suitcase-sized box under the table constructed of some off-white plastic with smooth surfaces and rounded corners. The mythical tradename ''Mr. Fusion'' came to mind.

''You see,'' the physician told them, ''I happened to be searching our records late last night for some technical clue which might prevent injuries like those I dealt with yesterday when I made the adventitious discovery of an important fact about the Elders. I believe it has a bearing not only on our respective missions here, but, I felt, on keeping the peace between us. So I summoned Eichra Oren and persuaded him that it must be shared with you.''

''Happened to be searching?'' Sam repeated cynically.

''Happened to be searching.'' Dlee Raftan Saon nodded back toward the computer which immediately sprang to life. So at least, Toya thought, it was implant controlled. A series of brief messages translated into English began to scroll across the monitor, sideways rather than bottom-to-top. More than anything, to Toya they resembled business and personal memos. In Soviet America, the age of government tolerance toward private computer bulletin boards had ended long before she'd been born. But the six-legged physician, it appeared, was far from finished with his explanation.

''I was performing a key-concept search on the message base, relative to these accidents we've been having, when the system alerted me to the existence of a pattern I had not anticipated.'' A faint, sweet scent, quite the opposite of what she would have expected, exuded from his body. ''It's there, to be sure, but it is subtle and elusive, consisting of tiny snippets, indirect references, asides in thousands upon thousands of communications between Mr. Thoggosh, his fellow nautiloids, and certain beings such as Scutigera.''

"Doesn't this kind of snooping violate the privacy customs of your own people?" Gutierrez asked.

"Certainly not," came the reply, a bit stiffly. His huge iridescent eyes glittered and his mouth parts worked nervously. "I was looking for technical conversation among our people here. Everything I discovered was posted publicly. The Elders simply aren't as discreet as they may prefer to believe. They're also fully as unaware of the revealing power of accumulated data as any human who ever had his fortune 'read' for him by one of your gypsies.''

"Well, it serves the Elders right," Toya suppressed a giggle. "They thought it was fine to intercept and decode—"

"Accidentally decode," Eichra Oren corrected. "They simply wrote their noise-elimination software too well.''

"Whatever," Toya responded with sarcastic impatience. "They were *our* transmissions to and from Earth, Eichra Oren. *Private* transmissions. Mr. Thoggosh brushed our objections aside. I wonder how he'll feel about having the same idea applied to him.''

"Good question, Toya," the Antarctican told her, "I remember other circumstances, other times, in which he'd think it was funny.''

"Yeah," Sam agreed, "he hasn't been himself lately. I wish he'd get back to it; nobody else wants the job." He leered and waggled his eyebrows.

"Sam, you've been watching old American movies again, haven't you?" Dlee Raftan Saon inquired. "Speaking of intercepting and decoding transmissions.''

"Why," asked the dog, "are my Groucho-marks showing?"

"Ahem . . ." The surgeon turned to look again as messages continued scrolling. Toya noticed that a word here, a phrase there, were marked, set apart from the rest in different colors. "You see, my friends, for as long as anyone can remember, the Elders believed themselves the earliest species ever to have evolved sapience on any alternative of Earth.''

Sam had placed his front paws on the table's edge and was peering into the screen. He imitated the surgeon's voice. ''Lately, however, they seem to have suffered an agonizing reappraisal of that opinion.''

''Relatively so,'' Dlee Raftan Saon answered, unaware of the impersonation. ''It's that plain? Dear me, I had to carry the process the next step, myself.'' Another nod and the messages vanished, leaving only the marked portions, sorted out by color, which began to assemble themselves into a document of their own. ''At any rate, now they seem to be searching desperately for some evidence of sapient beings they call the 'Predecessors.' ''

''It helps to carry more processing system around in your head, Dlee Raftan Saon.'' Sam looked up at Eichra Oren. ''One of the reasons for all the secrecy is that the Elders appear to be humiliated.''

''These Predecessors,'' Dlee Raftan Saon persisted, ''were a species unknown even to the Elders. There is, on the other hand, plenty of evidence for their having existed. Their artifacts, misidentified by most archaeologists, seem to be lying about practically everywhere.''

Toya interjected, ''What do you mean, 'everywhere'?''

Although he was no taller than Toya, his long, bobbing antennae bent over her, almost touching the top of her head. ''In each alternative universe the Elders discover, my dear, the Predecessors seem to have been there first.''

Gutierrez chuckled to himself. ''Kilroy was here.''

''I've heard that before,'' the girl told him. ''Corporal Owen said the same thing when we discovered that the Elders were here ahead of us.''

''Old joke,'' the general shook his head. ''Later, Toya.''

Dlee Raftan Saon raised a hairy manipulator. ''In at least one reality—and there is reason to believe it may have been more than one—they became Earth's predominant sapiencs long before nautiloids evolved. They rose to civilization, making every mistake any race makes and like their 'Successors' discovered an infinity of worlds of parallel probability. Like their Successors, they learned the secret of interdimensional travel.'' That brought exclamations from everyone. ''So far, they're the only other race within the explored realm of probability known to have achieved this impressive technical feat. It is that, of course, which makes our culture, the culture originally created by the Elders, so wealthy and diverse.''

The doctor pointed to one series of message fragments written in blue-purple lettering. ''The Predecessors seem to have taken a differing approach to multidimensional exploration, however. They never 'appropriated' the sapient inhabitants of other realities, for example.''

''Ethics already. That has to be an item,'' Sam offered, ''which galls our illustrious benefactors.''

''Of course, there weren't as many other sapients then. Certain other differences exist, as well,'' Dlee Raftan Saon went on, ''between the Elders and their unknown Predecessors, and their achievements. For one thing, the Predecessors enjoyed a lead of millions of years on their Successors.''

''Which means they weren't as bright as the Elders?''

The physician ignored the dog. ''For our culture, the culture of the Elders, interdimensional travel is still a risky, expensive, power-consuming undertaking, even after tens of thousands of years of research and practice.''

''Which means the Elders aren't as bright as the Predecessors.''

''Well, Sam,'' Dlee Raftan Saon acknowledged grudgingly, ''it does seem to be a source of humiliation with regard to the Predecessors, who appear to have been adept at slipping from one continuum to another. They made easier, more frequent use of interdimensional travel than we are able to do so far. Before the end, it had become a casual, everyday mode of travel to them, like driving a car once was to you Americans. Naturally, they left tantalizing traces of their culture spread throughout many coextant Solar Systems.''

Toya stepped toward the doctor. "And the end you mentioned?"

"My dear, despite their ubiquity, much time has passed and much has been destroyed by its passage. The Elders know little about the Predecessors, not even what they looked like. They have discovered one important fact—"

"They aren't around anymore," Sam suggested.

"Apparently by their own choosing. Eons ago, if I read these messages correctly, the Predecessors departed the System en masse, for the stars."

Momentary silence was filled with the sounds, outside, of heavy machinery and vehicles, an undertone that may have come from the drilling, the shouting of workers in a dozen languages, the voices of a dozen species. Above it all, Toya heard the whispery sound of another aerocraft passing over the worksite.

"Oops," the dog observed.

"You put it well, Sam. This discovery, as you anticipate, came as quite a shock to the Elders. It is characteristic of their culture that such a thing as traveling between the stars never occurred to them, and I believe they've always been inclined to dismiss similar ideas in currency among Appropriated Persons as the petty aspirations of, well, superstitious primitives—although they're far too polite to put it that way, of course."

Sam agreed, "They didn't even bring any ships of their own to this rock!"

"Indeed," replied the insect. "This does not, I'd have you understand, represent a great failing on the part of the Elders. Humans have an interest in going to the stars which the Elders never developed, but you never—or at least very seldom—thought about traveling to alternative universes."

"It's a matter," Toya decided out loud, "of a culturally shared mind-set."

"What do you mean?" the general asked her.

"Well, sir, Europeans in the Age of Discovery thought mostly about trade, conquest, and religious conversion.

Things like that never occurred to the Chinese at the height of their power. They impoverished themselves sending a vast fleet around the known world. Its sole purpose was to give gifts away to impress local rulers with China's magnificence.''

"In any event," continued Dlee Raftan Saon, "upon departing the Solar System, the Predecessors seem to have deliberately left behind the secret of their faster-than-light 'Virtual Drive.' ''

"It is meant," declared a voice they all recognized, *"as the inheritance of whatever Successor species eventually finds it."*

Five beings turned as one to face the tent door. Through it slithered a glistening twelve-foot snake which spoke with the voice of Mr. Thoggosh.

XVI
A Certain Uncertainty

"I see I've made what I fondly hope is an uncharacteristic error," the snake told them.

It was a separable "messenger" tentacle, outfitted for an excursion on land with a transparent plastic covering. Like a snake, it arranged one end in a supporting coil, raising the remainder of its length to human eye level. Unlike a snake, it tapered from that base, as thick as Toya's upper leg, to a finger-slender tip. She could see the dark patch of a thin-film transducer which was the electronic source of Mr. Thoggosh's voice.

Toya knew that originally a limb like this had evolved in

nautiloids, as it had in other cephalopods, as a specialized auxiliary sexual organ which detached itself from the owner's body to carry sperm to the female. In the Elders (who, like human beings, had changed their reproductive habits about the same time they'd developed sapience) it had become a sort of built-in "gofer," controlled by the same radio waves the nautiloids generated for speech. It was the organ to which Sam had been intended as an analog.

"So much," Mr. Thoggosh continued, *"for the well-laid plans of molluscs and men. I fear 'gang aft aglay' doesn't express the half of it. Preoccupied with what I foolishly believed my own safe secrets, I failed to perceive the figurative hot breath of two detectives on my even more figurative neck."*

Sam looked to Toya. Toya looked to Sam. Both wondered which of them had been left out of the Proprietor's calculations.

"Three detectives, sir," Eichra Oren offered, turning a palm up. "You simply made a mistake nonscientists often do, thinking of scientific fact as if it were some arcane ritual. You, more than anyone, should know that trade or defense secrets derived from objective reality never last long."

Gutierrez grinned and shook his head, but kept comment to himself.

"Indeed. Good afternoon, Dlee Raftan Saon, General Gutierrez." The tentacle slithered closer to the little group around the table. *"Toya, Eichra Oren, Sam, my congratulations to all three of you, then. Although I am scarcely to be blamed for such a mistake as you suggest if, in truth, I made it. Nautiloid physics and metaphysics have long been rooted in concepts which are often rather mystical-sounding to other sapients."*

The breeze blew the doorflap open and shut again, momentarily dazzling the eye. From somewhere outside, they heard the screech of protesting machinery, followed by the shouting of workers. It wasn't the first time they'd heard it, nor would it be the last.

"You're referring," the physician stretched three hands to the tabletop and switched his antique machinery off, "to the 'Twelve Elementals'?"

The tentacle tip bobbed affirmation. *"That I am, Raftan, although in point of fact, that magnificently breathtaking concept lies about as far from the realm of mysticism as it can and still relate to its primary context, the field of natural philosophy which our human guests call cosmology."*

More mechanical and vocal noise filtered in from outside. Toya wondered if they were having another of the failures that had plagued Mr. Thoggosh on this asteroid. Without being asked, Eichra Oren went to the back of the tent and began unstacking several folding objects of tubular metal and fabric which could be adjusted to support any one of a number of species. As soon as Gutierrez saw what he was doing, he went back to help.

"Refresh my memory on cosmology," the general asked over his shoulder, "if you don't mind."

The end of the appendage, bent at an angle, pointed at him. *"Gladly, sir. It's that field of intellectual inquiry concerned with the fundamental nature, especially the origin, of the universe. More than any other, it straddles the fence your people have mistakenly erected between the scientific discipline of physics and the philosophical discipline of metaphysics."*

"We humans can't do anything right." Gutierrez placed two folding chairs near the table. To match his sarcastic tone there was a skeptical look on his face. "You think there's something to that nonsense about reincarnation, extrasensory perception, spirit mediums, and crystal gazing?"

The tentacle conveyed a shudder. *"Dear me, I'd forgotten how badly contaminated the word has become on your world. Metaphysics, my dear fellow, is an ancient and honored discipline rather like cosmology, except that it asks, and tries to answer, questions about the fundamental nature of reality."*

"Reality"—Gutierrez sat beside Toya—"as opposed to 'the universe'?"

From Eichra Oren, Dlee Raftan Saon accepted a chair, folded in a different pattern to accommodate his insectile anatomy. He fished in a pocket of his labcoat and extracted an ordinary-looking briar pipe, stuffed it with what appeared to be tobacco, lit it, and puffed. Aromatic smoke filled the tent. "The difference, General, is subtle, but significant."

Gutierrez grinned and pulled a pack of smuggled cigarettes from his own breast pocket. Giving it a characteristically American toss, he offered one to Eichra Oren who shook his head politely. The Antarctican was sitting in a chair of his own, Sam on the floor at his knee as if he were an ordinary dog. Lighting a cigarette, the general said, "I'll take your word for it."

"*Very well,*" declared the tentacle, settling itself lower on a second coil, "*I suppose the place to begin, the first thing you should know, is that the shrewdest among our philosophers who concern themselves with the origin and nature of the universe are presently in my employ. You might say I've recently taken a sort of 'crash course' in the subject myself, although I'm still attempting to absorb the more slippery concepts involved. In any event, according to them, the universe possesses only six* known *fundamental forces.*"

"Is this anything human physics knows about?" Gutierrez inhaled smoke.

The surrogate gave the general another nod. "*Three are known as the 'Outer Forces,' familiar to you as gravity, magnetism, and electricity. Three more are the 'Inner Forces': the strong nuclear force, the weak nuclear force, and what is still to humanity a 'hidden' nuclear force, often, and erroneously, referred to as the 'fifth' force.*"

Gutierrez exhaled. "Why erroneously?"

"*The name, General, overlooks the epochal work of your own Michael Faraday or at least its cosmological significance. For you, the existence of this force has been inferred from other data. For us, it is an essential part of the machinery which brought us here. Together the two sets of forces, Inner and Outer, balance one another, creating an harmonious whole which your theorists would call symmetrical or 'beautiful'. . . ."*

"Beauty," Dlee Raftan Saon added, making clicking noises with his mouth parts which Toya knew signified amusement, "being in the optical receptor of the beholder." The insect-being drew on his pipe and exhaled a smoke ring, making Toya think of the hookah-smoking caterpillar in *Alice in Wonderland*.

"*Indeed*," responded Mr. Thoggosh with a trace of annoyance. "*Likewise, General, the universe has long been known to possess six dimensions. Three are the familiar dimensions of space: breadth, depth, and height. Three are dimensions of time, the first and most familiar of which we call 'duration.' The second is 'probability,' along which we all traveled, all of us except your party, to arrive on this asteroid.*"

"And the third?" Toya startled herself by blurting the question. Embarrassed, she sank back in her chair, determined not to interrupt again. Beside her, Eichra Oren gave her hand a reassuring touch.

The snakelike object standing in for Mr. Thoggosh was unperturbed. "*The third, Toya, remains unknown even to us. It is the 'hidden' dimension of time. Nobody knows quite what this last mysterious dimension might consist of, even (I might say 'especially') our philosophers, although they're certain it is something already familiar which everyone has overlooked.*"

"I'm not sure I understand, sir," Toya admitted, unable to help herself.

"*Well, reconsider the second dimension of time. Didn't your people wager with one another long before Monsieur Pascal formally discovered the laws of probability? I assure you that they did in my version of reality.*"

"Mine as well," the surgeon nodded, knocking his pipe out in an oddly shaped bowl he and Gutierrez had been sharing as an ashtray. Toya was sure it was some sort of bedpan. "In fact I'll wager that our guests would enjoy a bit of refreshment, perhaps even lunch. Is anyone else as hungry as I am?"

For a few minutes, the dissertation on metaphysics and cosmology was interrupted as their orders were relayed to the camp caterer via implant. The general put his cigarette out and asked for a cheeseburger, knowing it was a dish the nautiloids had recently discovered. Toya asked the physician to make it two. Sam and Eichra Oren sent their own requests. Whatever energy it drew from Mr. Thoggosh's body, the appendage was incapable of refueling itself and continued lecturing while they waited for lunch.

"These two pairs of three forces and three dimensions comprise the twelve known 'Elementals.' Just as we have found the hidden nuclear force, as your scientists have not yet, we all fondly hope to find the hidden dimension of time on 5023 Eris. It is believed by some, having done that, that we may discover another set of six—or even twelve—'hidden' Elementals."

Before anyone could ask him to explain, the meal arrived in insulated boxes carried by trainable insectile nonsapients. Except for their number of limbs, they bore little resemblance to the highly sapient Dlee Raftan Saon. Food was distributed as Mr. Thoggosh went on.

"Which it will be, six, twelve, or none, is the subject of the most sanguine debate since those culminating in the Great Restitution. Careers are made, unmade, and remade every day depending on who's currently winning. Lifelong friends are known to stop speaking for centuries. It doesn't seem to matter that, so far, there are no hard facts to base opinion on."

"Just like academics back home," Gutierrez observed around a bite of burger. Like Toya, he held the plastic container on his lap. The sandwich had come with lettuce, tomato, and onion. Nor were french fries forgotten. A tall glass of lemonade stood beside his elbow on the computer table.

"Regrettably so. I even know of a duel fought over the subject."

"Now *there's* an idea for establishing priority!" Gutierrez laughed. Toya was unsure what he found so funny. "What do you think it is, six or twelve?"

"I've no idea, General. However it turns out, these new Elementals are likely to be arrayed in either two or four subsets of three Elementals each, bringing the universe into full symmetry. These extra Elementals, like the hidden time dimension, can possibly be inferred from the workings of the Predecessors' Virtual Drive, understanding and operation of which, it seems, depends on accepting an even more bizarre idea."

He waited for some reaction. Eichra Oren's attention seemed to be on his food, some unrecognizable but vaguely Chinese-looking dish. Sam was eating the same sort of thing from a container on the floor. Toya's hamburger was better than anything she'd ever had back home. She couldn't bring herself to examine too closely whatever Dlee Raftan Saon was sucking through the tube he'd inserted in one side of his food container. She was certain that all three were in fact focused intently on the nautiloid's words.

"Mass, as such, my associates inform me, doesn't really exist. Unlike the question of how many Elementals there are, nobody in the philosophical community seems to disagree with this idea, which, I confess, seems ridiculous to me. Subatomic particles, they say, are merely probabilistic ripples on the matrix of space-time. This includes, of course, those particles comprising sapient beings who wish to travel from place to place."

Sam looked up from his place. "How's that?" It was the first time Toya had seen him eating and she understood now why he was shy about it. Lacking hands, he was reduced by the process to the animal nature he'd transcended.

The tentacle leaned over to address the dog. *"As I*

understand it, Oasam, quantum physics holds that these particles are just as statistically likely to do their rippling in one place as in another. However intelligent and curious one may be, the concept almost makes one's brain ache."

"In other words," the dog offered, "if a particle can exist 'here'—"

"By which you mean the traveler's presumed point of departure . . ."

"Right—then why not over 'there'?" Sam lowered his head to lap some liquid from a compartment of his plate.

"His intended destination?" The tentacle assumed a twisted posture, then relaxed. *"According to physics, the two phenomena amount to the same thing. In theory, getting 'there' should be no greater problem than simply staying 'here.' And after all, people and other objects seem to do the latter on a regular basis without much difficulty, don't they?"*

"Zen teleportation." Eichra Oren spoke for the first time in a while. "What you're saying, sir, is that the Predecessors traveled from one place to another more or less simply by changing the way they looked at things."

"And a pinch of pixie dust," Sam suggested.

Mr. Thoggosh's answer began with a long pause. *"One of the difficulties I find with this concept, gentlebeings, and I assure you I find many, is that it sounds suspiciously like a free lunch. Over the course of a long career and an even longer lifetime, I've learned to distrust such propositions."*

"Still, if it were true," Dlee Raftan Saon mused, "it would be a wonderful thing, brimming with possibility."

"Indeed, Raftan. The concept, you see, doesn't involve real acceleration or its concomitant and rather inconvenient relativistic effects. It seems to be a matter of avoiding the speed of light, rather than exceeding it."

"Better yet," Sam suggested, "from a businessman's point of view, the process consumes no fuel."

"The thought had occurred to me, yes," replied the mollusc. *"Theory to one side for the time being, and from a*

strictly practical standpoint, things haven't been going smoothly for our enterprise here, which is why I've decided to tell you all the full truth and enlist your aid."

XVII
Hope of Redemption

"Geronimo, John Galt, this is *Laika.* Check your throttles again. My line feels slack, regardless of what the tension readouts tell me. Over."

Horatio Gutierrez, former AeroSpace Force brigadier general, officer in charge of the American Soviet Socialist Republic's expedition to the asteroid 5023 Eris, still captain of the twice-refitted and renamed space shuttle once known as the *Daniel P. Moynihan,* peered out the left seat window at two other spacecraft, identical to his own, where they strained under their respective loads against a star-flecked background of blackest velvet. He'd never have believed it possible two weeks ago, but it felt good to be in space again, even if it meant resuming command of the small fleet of "Polish bombers" that in so many ways were the exact opposite of the sleek Soviet American interceptors he'd spent most of his life flying.

"Geronimo *here,* Laika. *We copy."* The voice of Major Jesus Ortiz, captain of the former *James C. Wright,* issued from a speaker overhead. *"This goofball of ours claims we're three-hundredths of one percent overthrottled. I repeat, zero-point-zero-three. I'm attempting to correct now. Over."*

"John Galt *to* Laika," added Lieutenant Colonel Juan

Sebastiano, captain of the former *Howard M. Metzenbaum*. *"Our goofball's telling the same story. I'm not sure our control's that fine, but we'll give it a try. Over."*

The "feel" Gutierrez referred to was more a matter of how the modified engines sounded than any tension reading or velocity indication. He was too preoccupied even to spare a glance at the computer, one of three onboard which now struck him as primitive. Projecting from it, the alien interface Mr. Thoggosh had supplied (in the same casual way his chemists had cooked up the needed fuel) looked like a head-sized gray-green fungus. It had been created to help *Laika* and her sisters complete a mission which, like the expedition itself, they'd never been designed for. Hooked into the nautiloid cybernet, the "goofball," as his crew were calling it, performed calculations necessary to insert a miniature moon into orbit around the miniature planet. His own goofball told him, through a telltale on the already crowded control board, that his adjustments were perfect. Gutierrez didn't trust it.

Trailing on impossibly slender cables ten kilometers behind the craft (although in another sense they were trailing it as it preceded them in orbit) was a mountain of silica which would have been a kilometer in diameter had it been remotely spherical. To Gutierrez it resembled nothing in particular. It was about twice as long as it was thick, peppered with tiny impact craters. One curving surface was almost smooth except for a large elongated astrobleme (he'd thought craters weren't supposed to form like that) which was the most remarkable feature of the unremarkable rock. What was important was that it was the correct mass and composition. They'd found it, as Aelbraugh Pritsch had suggested they would, within a thousand kilometers, the average distance between asteroids in this region of the Belt.

Had it been only a week since Mr. Thoggosh had confessed, during that remarkable conversation in Dlee Raftan Saon's tent, how weary he was of equipment failures and other technical problems associated with a groundsearch for the

Predecessor artifacts he was looking for? Looking back, it seemed much longer. What he wanted to do, he'd told the general, was place a smaller asteroid in a polar orbit around 5023 Eris. He'd reassured Gutierrez that, given technology available to the Elders, such an undertaking was by no means impossible. There was no lack of small rocks circling the Sun in this orbit and many were within easy reach of the nautiloid establishment.

"In aid of what, I suspect you are about ask," the appendage had responded to the general's upraised eyebrows. *"Quite simply, I plan to establish an unbeinged base on our semiartificial moonlet. At that range, it can be directed quite as efficiently as one of our aerostats."*

Gutierrez had grimaced, then laughed. He'd ridden here aboard one of the machines Mr. Thoggosh was talking about. So had the tentacle, for that matter. Both were parked just outside the door. Gutierrez had long since gathered that, had some calamity happened to the appendage, the mollusc could grow another, however long it took or painful it might be. He'd have a much tougher time growing himself a new Horatio, he thought with a morbid grin.

"It's the next step, General, no more impossible than the rest, I assure you, which takes one's intellectual breath away. We have in our possession certain instruments, new even to our science, which collect and interpret the galaxy's natural background neutrino flux. They were imposed upon me at the outset of our expedition by certain individuals with a greater and more detachedly scientific interest in this affair than my own. They believe that each alternative universe has its own unique neutrino pattern. Now I'm rather grateful they were so adamant."

Gutierrez had listened as Mr. Thoggosh explained to Dlee Raftan Saon (whose specialization lay in areas other than physics), that neutrinos were subatomic particles so small and swift they could pass through anything, including an entire planet, almost as if it weren't there. During the course of this explanation it had developed that the word "almost" (statistically a few neutrinos would be stopped or slowed by dense objects they attempted to pass through) was critical to the scheme.

"As these elusive particles pass, or fail to pass, through the world we occupy, which possesses roughly the same surface area as the region known as 'Texas,' these captured neutrinos will create, in effect, a spiraling X ray or CAT scan of the entire globe. This three-dimensional pattern of relative transmission and absorption will be detected on our little moon and relayed to our imaging and translating computers." The latter were devices that had accidentally broken Earth's most sophisticated military codes, having mistaken them for naturally occurring interference. *"Since neutrinos are very small themselves,"* Mr. Thoggosh had concluded, *"resolution should be excellent."*

"Giving us a peek," Dlee Raftan Saon suggested, "at what's inside."

"Precisely." Bent at the tip, the tentacle had given the impression it was turning to look at each of them. *"I cannot bring myself to believe that the Predecessors, having taken care to leave so many tantalizing clues behind, would have made the task of recovering their technological legacy as difficult as it's seemed. Such a scan should reveal any great masses beneath the surface, including the object of our search, and possibly a method of getting to it. I can stop wasting my time, my investors' money, and the colony's dwindling supply of equipment on all this confounded blind drilling."*

At this point the surrogate had turned to Gutierrez. *"I believe this plan to be effective, General, but it's hindered by a lack of spacecraft to move the requisite small asteroid. I confess it was not a necessity I anticipated when I planned this expedition more than a century ago."*

Gutierrez had nodded, "I assume you can't just send for a spaceship."

"Well, sir," Mr. Thoggosh replied, *"I've always been*

reluctant to employ, without the direst necessity, the expensive and somewhat unreliable facilities for interdimensional transport we have at our disposal. In this instance, both the difficulty and the expense increase as a function of the fifth power of the longest dimension of whatever's being sent."

"So it's especially dangerous to bring something as large as a ship?"

"And expensive." Even through a voice transducer, irony was audible in the nautiloid's chuckle. *"What made the task appear insurmountable was the utter impossibility I anticipated of accomplishing what I believe necessary under your watchful eye, sir. Thinking of you Americans, however, gave me an idea. You have have the spacecraft, even if—I, er, that is . . ."*

"Even if they're primitive by standards you're used to?"

Again the chuckle. *"You've said it, sir, so I shan't have to. Might it be possible, I thought, given appropriate consideration, to borrow one or two of your craft and the crewbeings necessary to operate them?"*

The general had laughed. "It wouldn't be unprecedented. It would be like people from our civilization borrowing a canoe from Pacific natives to recover the nose cone of a downed satellite. But you couldn't do it, could you, without giving the purpose of the search away?"

The transducer had transmitted the sound of a sigh which Gutierrez knew to be affectation. The marine mollusc, a relative to the squid and octopus, breathed silently through gills. *"I confess, Horatio, had I been human I'd have shaken my head with the futility of it all. The canoe analogy occurred to me. It appeared to have ominous implications. If I recall correctly, primitives who use them are likely to be headhunters or cannibals."*

It was the first time Mr. Thoggosh had called him by his given name and it felt friendly even if it was a sales pitch. Gutierrez had been about to reply that he didn't care for calamari, but wasn't sure how it would be taken.

"From the long, terrible experience of my own people,"

Mr. Thoggosh had continued, *"I knew that there's more than one kind of cannibalism. Sapients are as easily consumed by taxation or conscription as in a black iron stewpot. I shuddered, indeed I still shudder, to think of the immoral uses your governments might make of the Predecessors' impressive technology."*

"Yet datum by datum," Eichra Oren had interrupted, "you realized you were inevitably losing the hopeless struggle to maintain secrecy."

Sam had added, "You weren't surprised at all by our uncovering your secrets, were you, you old fake?"

"Only by how quickly it was done. No need to be so harsh, Otusam—put yourself in my place. I was aware that, with your help, against my explicit wishes, Eichra Oren was continuing his investigation." The appendage had swiveled back to the general. *"The stubborn fellow defined learning my secrets as a necessary part of the task I'd assigned him. I was forced to concede, to myself, that he'd a measure of logic and justice on his side."*

"Logic and justice," Eichra Oren had observed, "amount to the same thing."

"Well," Mr. Thoggosh had gone on, *"there wasn't much I could do short of firing him. Not only would that involve me in the difficulty and expense of shipping him home, his mother, an old and esteemed friend, would likely never speak to me again."* Mr. Thoggosh had sighed again. *"On the other appendage, whatever Eichra Oren discovered, an observant and rather frightened Sergeant Pulaski would soon learn, as well."*

Sitting up suddenly, Toya had opened her mouth in reflexive denial. Mr. Thoggosh had ignored her.

"She, I knew, reports directly to you, Horatio. This saves a shy and nervous little female the emotional strain of dealing with less sympathetic superiors. You, sir, report to the American KGB's own Mr. Empleado. He, in turn, reports to the mysterious secret Russian agent, Iron Butterfly."

This time Gutierrez had laughed and slapped a knee,

shaking his head in surprised amusement. "I only regret that Art isn't around to hear that!"

"*But he is,*" Mr. Thoggosh had corrected, "*just outside, at the back of the tent. Iron Butterfly's watching him through binoculars from the edge of the gulch. No matter: the time lag represented by this layered method of communication was less than a couple of your hours. Left to itself, a quiet but rather desperate race would soon develop between our two groups, human and nautiloid. Despite any superficial cordiality we somehow managed to maintain between ourselves, it would be an all-out struggle. Who would find, understand, and employ the Predecessors' Virtual Drive first? And it was this string of expectations which made my mind up.*"

Ignoring the urge to run out and drag the damnable secret operative from the bushes, Gutierrez had fished in a coverall pocket for his cigarettes, pulled one out, and lit it. "A while back you said 'given appropriate consideration.' Did you have anything specific in mind?"

It was Mr. Thoggosh's turn for a thoughtful pause, although he'd lacked the excuse afforded by a cigarette. "*Well, sir, as you know, we're reluctant to deal with your governments—let's make that 'unwilling'—whatever the cost. Nevertheless, each of our groups has motivations of its own, rather I should say that each of us as individuals does, and sometimes they're shared by others in the group—consistent with our own peculiar necessities.*"

Gutierrez had looked at the messenger shrewdly. "And?"

"*And those referred to as 'the Elders,' including myself, feel a degree of humiliation at what we now see as our lack of imagination and progress.*"

The general had leaned forward. "I'm not sure I follow you."

"*You will, Horatio. I'm being as open as I know how to be. True, we independently inferred the existence of alternative reality. Using this esoteric knowledge, we invented (or*

*with reference to our Predecessors, I should say unknowingly
reinvented) interdimensional travel."*

"Okay so far." Gutierrez had grinned, struck with the
necessity of reassuring an ancient and accomplished being
who suddenly seemed hesitant and doubtful. "Watch it on
the corners, though."

*"I shall. We even have a healthy interplanetary com-
merce in our version of the System, mostly carried out, I'm
chagrined to confess, by Appropriated Persons. For millions
of years we've had astronomers and are well aware of the
size, shape, and composition of the galaxy around us. Yet it
never occurred to us to physically explore interstellar space."*

Gutierrez had asked Toya, "The cultural viewpoint thing,
right?"

The girl had nodded back, shyly.

"We fervently hope," Mr. Thoggosh had told them, *"To
redeem ourselves by following in the Predecessors' wake. I
feel I can trust you to help us, because I believe I know
what you want."*

"And what," Gutierrez had asked him, "is that?"

*"With what you learn here, you exiled Americans simply
hope to buy yourselves a ticket home."*

XVIII
Fear of Confrontation

Aimlessly, Mr. Thoggosh wandered through the garden of
tactile sculpture he maintained in the forefront of his office,
letting his tentacles trail across each piece without feeling
the contours beneath them.

Filled with a quantity of metabolic carbon dioxide, the great shell that housed his body hovered a meter above the sandy floor. A less ponderous being than he appeared, he had always been lighter on his metaphorical feet then he let the Americans realize. Now he wondered if he should drop that pose for the benefit of his next visitors.

The truth, he thought bitterly, *won't always set you free*. He'd known, following the conference in Dlee Raftan Saon's tent, that he'd soon find himself with an angry moral debt assessor on his metaphorical hands. He'd decided that when it happened, it would be his own fault, a price he had to pay to attain his ultimate objective. That it had taken Eichra Oren a week to make this appointment—ostensibly because he must help his fellow humans rearrange their camp so the shuttles could be used to capture a moon—only served as a measure of the man's annoyance.

Eichra Oren had every right to be annoyed. Security restrictions such as those he'd initially imposed here were unheard of in the world of the nautiloids and their associates. They'd long since proven more expensive (economically and in a sense that went beyond economic considerations, crossing into personal dignity and liberty) than anything preserved by them. Having imposed them nonetheless, he couldn't, in all justice, blame Eichra Oren for resenting their sudden and complete abandonment.

His implant chirped a message from Aelbraugh Pritsch. His guests had been processed through the airlock—they had filled their respiratory systems with the same oxygenated fluorocarbon liquid he swam in—and were waiting outside his office. Sending his assent, he pivoted in midfluid to return to the area that served him as a desk, then thought better of it and decided to break all precedent by greeting them at the door.

When the pressure-panel slid aside, in addition to Eichra Oren he saw Sam (whose furry coat made him hate plunging himself into the liquid that filled Mr. Thoggosh's quarters) and Toya Pulaski. At his invitation they preceded him toward the back of the office and sat in chairs—all but Sam—which lowered themselves from the ceiling while he arranged himself behind his "desk."

Behind him, against a starry background incongruous in the depths of his live-in aquarium, a wall display set up for the benefit of his Soviet American visitors showed the progress of the mission in space from the vantage of Gutierrez's flagship, the *Laika*.

"It's good to see you here, my—"

"Skip the amenities, Mr. Thoggosh," Eichra Oren declared. "I came to hand in our resignation, mine and Sam's. We might work for an employer who lies to us. 'Truth is a valuable commodity you don't automatically owe to everyone.' But we won't work—I won't work—for someone who gives us a job and then undoes it himself without any warning."

"Me neither," Sam added.

"I see," replied the nautiloid. "What will you do instead?"

The Antarctican frowned. "We'd go home, but I understand your reluctance to use the interdimensional transporter too casually. My quarters are on your land and grew from a seed you provided. I suppose, until enough good reasons accumulate to use the transporter, I'll vacate them and throw in with Toya's people. Don't worry, it isn't your obligation anymore."

Mr. Thoggosh lifted tentacles in a sinuous shrug. "I believe you're mistaken. I promised I'd compensate you whether you worked or not, until I get you back to our continuum. Your quarters are part of that compensation. I'll keep the rest of my promise, if you'll permit me."

Eichra Oren opened his mouth to protest. Mr. Thoggosh hurried on before he could utter a word. "I'd like to ask you a procedural question, however. You feel you have a grievance against me. I'll concede it for the sake of discussion. If I wished to make appropriate restitution, Eichra Oren, how would I go about it, since you're the only debt assessor on the asteroid?''

"Watch it, Boss," Sam warned. "He's soaping it up to stick it to you!"

The man leaned back and put a hand under his chin. "You could wait until this is over and we can settle the debt back home."

Not for the first time, Mr. Thoggosh wished he could shake his head. "If we succeed here, I may not return. Besides, the Americans have a saying: 'Justice delayed is justice denied.' You'll acknowledge that this applies to a moral debtor who wishes to rebalance the scales as much as to a creditor?"

"For the sake of discussion. What do you suggest?"

"That, in absence of another debt assessor, I rely on your faculties in an attempt to explain my actions. Possibly you'll feel afterward that I don't owe you a debt. If not, I'll accept any judgment you care to levy."

Eichra Oren raised his eyebrows. "Any judgment?"

"Did I speak too softly? Any judgment. I'll abandon this project and take everyone home if you insist. You have my solemn word of honor."

Eichra Oren was visibly taken aback. "I'll listen."

Mr. Thoggosh laid one tentacle over another and began to relax for the first time in days. "Very well, you heard something of my concerns last week when I spoke with General Gutierrez about borrowing his spacecraft. Primarily I feared that a human government might get hold of Predecessor technology. That, you can appreciate, is something to be very much afraid of."

"*Mister* Gutierrez," Sam corrected. "His commission expired when he agreed to help you. The reason his people didn't replace him, or put him against a wall and shoot him, is that they're all as fed up with their government, most of them anyway, as he is, and agreed with him it was a good idea."

The nautiloid suppressed annoyance. "I was under an

impression that military rank would be retained as an aid to efficient operation. But I was explaining myself.'' He turned to the Antarctican. ''When I gave you your assignment, I did not wish to burden a valuable employee with my deepest fears. I worried that it might affect your, er, spontaneity, interfere with your all-important attempt to get to know the other humans on this asteroid better. Especially''—he gave Toya what he hoped was a look of appreciation—''the increasingly knowledgeable and dangerous Sergeant Pulaski.''

''That much,'' the man responded guardedly, ''I understand.''

''Also, there was the embarrassing matter of what I felt—still feel—are the failures of my own species. Perhaps I fell short of candor, but I wasn't anxious for others to know how dull witted the 'Elders' have been.''

With what the humans might have called a sinking circulatory organ, the nautiloid suddenly realized that everything he was saying sounded perfectly idiotic. He hoped Eichra Oren would see through that to the real message he wanted to convey. He allowed the empty spaces in his shell to fill with air, gradually rising until he floated a few inches above the floor. To his right, at a signal from his implant, the door to his personal quarters slid aside.

''But come—I've something that should be of particular interest to the sergeant. We can continue our conversation under pleasanter auspices.''

He encouraged them to follow him through the door and with an enthusiasm he knew was transparently proprietary welcomed them into his apartment. He'd adjusted the light to suit them. To him, descended from deep-sea creatures as he was, his familiar quarters were filled with glare, as if they were arc lit. There was little any human being would have recognized as furniture. In one corner stood a high-sided bed of carefully cleaned and sifted sand where he slept. On a sort of night table he'd set his favorite piece of tactile sculpture. It bore no visual resemblance to anything real (this being an important part of the artistic effort), but was immediátely recognizable to nautiloid tentacles as a particularly seductive female of his own species.

"I've brought you to see my own collection of Predecessor artifacts."

Scattered about were the more mundane objects Mr. Thoggosh had everyday use for, books in different media, writing implements, portraits of friends and relatives. Instruments for cleaning and grooming himself sat on a shelf below what humans might have recognized as a mirror, had they been capable of seeing in the same spectrum of frequencies nautiloids used. Even to Eichra Oren, who knew what it was, it looked like a dully polished sheet of metal. Their host invited them to sit on the floor, deeply covered with yet another grade of soft, fine sand.

"One reason," he continued as before, "I kept my search a secret for so long was out of simple consideration for others. The last thing I wanted was to get everyone unduly excited about the possibilities here."

Sam yawned pointedly and settled to the floor. "Gimme a break."

Mr. Thoggosh ignored him. "It wasn't just a matter of the gamble I had persuaded Scutigera and the others to take with me. They're sophisticated investors, well aware of the risks involved in any such undertaking. It was really a much more intangible matter of the morale of an entire civilization—I needn't add that the self-esteem of the nautiloid species is involved, as well." He lifted a tentacle. "Just look at the objects in this display case and you'll see what I mean."

"Excuse me, Mr. Thoggosh," Toya asked, "but what display case?"

He laid a tentacle on what Eichra Oren had taken for another mirror. "What's transparent to one eye may not be to another." He opened the panel and removed a couple of small objects which he passed to the humans.

Eichra Oren nodded without comment as he accepted one of the objects and Toya examined another. Everything Mr. Thoggosh handed them appeared delicate. Each appeared to have been formed randomly of some ceramic substance, yet, at the same time, seemed made for some specific purpose.

"That's a common sort we find on various versions of Earth, though this one's from here. A kind of wrench, I think," Mr. Thoggosh told Toya. "The irregular taper within the crescent fits a knob seen on larger artifacts. We've never been able to turn those, with our own tools or even with tools like this, but such devices applied to simulations turn them without effort, as if there were a motor inside. I think it's a sort of lever to convert whatever force you apply to rotary motion. It's all of a piece and contains no separate or moving parts. It also makes musical notes when subjected to anything over six tonnes of torque."

"Six tonnes?" Seated on the floor with her legs crossed, Toya looked up at the Elder. "But it seems so fragile."

"Do anything you wish, my dear. Such remnants prove, under all but the most strenuous tests known to mechanics, completely indestructible."

Eichra Oren held his own object up, a disk four centimeters in diameter, transparent to the human eye—he wondered whether Mr. Thoggosh knew that—with extensions of the same material, shaped a bit like antennae. It looked as if it were made of lace—glass lace—two millimeters thick, yet he couldn't bend it, let alone break it. Deep within its illusionary center, there appeared to be vague movement and light.

"We don't know what that is," confided Mr. Thoggosh, "except that it must be locked away. It interferes with certain radio frequencies and some chemical reactions refuse to occur in its presence. You'll appreciate that I don't look forward to sifting the soil of 5023 Eris a cubic meter at a time for any more such. Yet if we hadn't solved the drilling problem, that's exactly what we'd have had to do."

Drifting over the bed, Mr. Thoggosh settled himself. "There are other objects in the cabinet if you care, but they're all trivial so far. What might yet be discovered is without precedent in the history of known civilization. Only

the exploration of alternate worlds fails to pale by compari-
son. Had I disappointed everyone, I might have incurred a
moral debt to them. I wasn't certain anyone knows how to
pay such a unique debt or that even a *p'Nan* debt assessor
would be able to figure it out.''

Having grown up in the same culture as Mr. Thoggosh,
Eichra Oren shared his ethical values, along with the uncer-
tainties they sometimes produced. For that and other reasons
he was beginning to see some sense in Mr. Thoggosh's
explanation. Such an attitude was easier to assume, of
course, now that he knew his employer's secret anyway.

"We've known each other a long time," the mollusc told
him. "All of your relatively short life. I've known your
esteemed mother, Eneri Relda, even longer. We've been
friends the majority of her remarkable fifteen-thousand-year
lifespan. We were first introduced when she was a girl just
snatched from disaster and I little more than a freshly
hatched egg.''

The dog yawned. "Is all this ancient history headed
somewhere?''

"Dealing with humans, I often ask myself what Eneri
Relda would do. Since my secret would soon be out—I'm
relieved no longer to have the burden of protecting it—and
there was no way of getting it back, I thought it of
paramount importance to reach some sort of agreement as
quickly as possible with General Gutierrez which would
preclude his government's interference.''

"Hmm." The assessor looked at the paleontologist. "What
you don't know, what I didn't see any reason to tell you
since you were holding out on me, was that Toya and I
came to a similar agreement. She's decided she prefers the
society created by you Elders to the one she grew up in.''

"Yes," the girl responded diffidently, "I remembered your
offer, Mr. Thoggosh. I found myself regretting that I didn't
take it. I decided I'd tell them nothing that might endanger
your project, whatever it was. Or your culture's ability to
defend itself from the United World Soviet.''

Eichra Oren grinned. "I thought Toya's attitude was sensible. I told her I'd do my best to find a place for her when this was over with. She believed we could trust Gutierrez. He seemed to be coming to the same conclusions she had and wouldn't pass on dangerous information to the KGB."

Mr. Thoggosh grunted. "I can't say I blame you for failing to allay my fears. Our mutual trust of the general is borne out by his cooperation, and in the way he renamed his spacecraft and allowed the others to be renamed by their respective captains. Geronimo I've heard of, but you'll have to fill me in on the other, Toya. Who is John Galt?"

She shook her head. "Colonel Sebastiano won't tell anybody." She still hadn't lost the habit of glancing around to see if anyone dangerous was listening. "I think it's from some movie that was suppressed."

"I see. Well, it's time we came to an agreement ourselves, Eichra Oren. May we assume that something resembling peace exists between us once again?"

Eichra Oren nodded. "I think we can assume that, yes."

"Because, unlike Toya here, and General Gutierrez, some Americans have yet to reach a resolution to their problems. First and foremost, especially for individuals like Mr. Empleado, is the question of survival. I want you to make sure that, whatever solution he arrives at, it doesn't imperil our own."

XIX
Streetlights and Matches

Away, away, we're bound for the mountain,
Bound for the mountain, bound for the mountain,

> Over the hill, the wildwoods acallin',
> Away to the chase, away, away!

"I seem to recall," Rosalind remarked as she scuffed through the leafy debris of the forest floor, "that the name of that song is 'Cumberland Mountain Deer Chase.' I thought we were hunting wild pigs."

Betal grinned back and slapped at the pistol thrust into his coverall pocket. "Yes, ma'am, but I don't know any pig-hunting songs."

A few paces behind, Danny and a companion enjoyed the good-natured banter. "Each day it's harder to believe Betal was a KGB thug."

"One of Empleado's 'enforcers'?" Dlee Raftan Saon asked.

"Yes, that beating seems to have done him a world of good."

"Call me Raftan. Today I am not a healer, but a hunter. For my part, I find it equally hard to believe that your delicate-looking physician insisted on coming with us for more than merely medical reasons."

Danny laughed. "She grew up on her grandfather's tales of stalking tigers and monkeys and God knows what else in the 'old country.' Now she wants to try it herself."

He doubted whether the Marine-issue CZ99A1s she and Betal both carried, chambered in .41x22m/m, were adequate for the boar described by their "native guide." Glancing at the stainless .44 in his own hand, he realized he didn't have much confidence in the stopping power of the short-barreled S&W his father had left with him. But they were going to have a hell of a good time finding out, and maybe bring back some roasting pork as a bonus.

It was hard to tell who was in charge. Dr. Nguyen relied for whatever authority she needed on her medical degree. Danny couldn't remember whether she rated bars or oak leaves. Betal had a commission, but it was probably classified. Marna was next in line, but she'd signed on as a techie and like most of the party had never hunted before. She carried the same Mini-30, a carbine in 7.62x39m/m Russian, they'd been issued in basic training.

"You're right to wonder," he told Raftan. "In our culture, hunting's sneered at and discouraged." By an aristocracy of wine-and-cheese leftists, he thought to himself, who'd converted America into a Marxist state a century ago and continued to rule despite claims it was the ultimate democracy.

The physician chuckled. "Only someone who has never gone hungry disdains hunting." Well, Danny thought, the one promise socialist egalitarianism had kept was that everyone had the same chance—slim and none except for the Volvo *nomenklatura*—at three meals a day. "In our culture," Dlee Raftan Saon added, "it's valued, among other reasons, because it's the only thing, besides sapience itself, that all our species have in common."

Danny felt his eyebrows lift. "Even mobile veggies like whatshername?"

"Why do you think they became mobile? For a number of excellent reasons, all sapients begin as predators."

That would bear thinking about. It certainly explained, Danny thought, why things like wild boars had been included in the terraforming process. In part, this asteroid was a game preserve!

As a second lieutenant, he supposed he came next in rank, but any claim he made to bossing this effort would seem silly beside the credentials of its three lowest-ranking members. It turned out that his nominee for Most Useless Crewman, Staff Sergeant C. C. Jones, had actually done some hunting, illegally, growing up as a country boy. That was probably reflected in his choice of weapon, one of the mission's Remington Model 1100 12-gauge semiautomatic riot guns, now loaded with enormous solid slugs. Corporal Roger Owen, another individual of rustic background, carried a Mini-30. Corporal Carlos "Rubber Chicken" Alvarez, cook and garbage disposer, rounded out the trio of experienced hunters with another Remington.

As the party made its way through the woods the three betrayed their past crimes another way, swapping yarns about the power and ferocity of wild pigs they'd hunted before. For Owen it had been javelina in New Mexico, "almost too fast to draw a bead on." Jones and Alvarez had hunted—and apparently been hunted by—things called "razorbacks," capable of absorbing dozens of bullets without serious damage and hamstringing opponents with their sharp, side-reaching tusks. Danny had always thought of pigs as cute little pink things with curly tails which tended to stutter when they got excited.

"There's no finesse to this," Owen had warned him. "These animals are territorial and mean as hell. We'll just spread out, stomp through their front yard, and when they show up to eject trespassers—pork chops!"

"Or long pig," Alvarez had chuckled.

Jones had nodded. "Always that possibility." He almost seemed to relish the idea. Danny had gulped and done his best to look intrepid.

The three conferred with Tl*m*nch*l, who had already hunted here and acted as their guide. He appeared to have a few yarns of his own. No one seemed to mind that the humans had begun supplementing their rapidly dwindling rations by foraging in the "super kudzu" forest. Mr. Thoggosh, making the point through his birdlike assistant, had insisted that they hunt only with guides at first. Otherwise, they might kill and eat some sapient no human had seen before. There was no lack of individuals willing to sacrifice themselves, on company time, by hunting with the humans to prevent such a tragedy. Tl*m*nch*l carried a boxy weapon on his equipment belt. His companion, introduced as Dr*f*rst*v, was trying his luck with a Mini-30, like a human hunter opting sportingly for a muzzle loader or a bow.

But, as Danny explained, there was more involved in this

trip than sport. "Since arriving on the asteroid, we Americans have enjoyed what amounts to an all-expenses-paid vacation. Without lifting a finger, we're supplied with adequate water, warmth, shelter, and more than ample elbowroom."

"Sweet streams flow freely," the physician replied, "and the air—"

"Is unpolluted," Danny suggested, "unlike that of the world most of us wish, perversely enough, to get back to."

"While overhead, the Elders' canopy protects you from the rigors of space. All of this bounty, my friend, is a simple, unavoidable by-product of arrangements which the Elders and their friends have provided for themselves."

"Yeah. So I understand."

Until now, for protection from weather under the canopy, they'd had the venerable spaceships—and shelter beneath their wings—that had brought them here. For the time being they were gone, lifted in the baskets that had lowered them to the surface, on a mission to give 5023 Eris a moon. But even the Elders' makeshift was better than Earth's best. In addition to the cargo-bay passenger inserts, removed from the shuttles to make room for internal fuel tanks and set up in the encampment on the equivalent of concrete blocks, self-heating and self-cleaning tents stood where the spacecraft had been. Everyone now had the privacy they hadn't enjoyed since taking off from Earth, in some cases, since they'd been born. That was probably why two or three women were whispering about missed periods and tender breasts, although Rosalind maintained that it was too early to tell. Few seemed unhappy about any of it, pregnancy included. Eventually, they'd been promised, they'd get their precious ships back. Aelbraugh Pritsch had told them they could keep the tents, as well.

"Although Owen's making noises about building a log cabin."

The insect chuckled again. "So your needs are taken care

of by individualistic, capitalistic aliens better than any socialist regime on Earth has ever been able to do.''

''That's right. We're getting a free ride on their incidental surplus.''

''Let me tell you, young friend: as you've observed, the Elders enjoy a half-billion-year lead in areas philosophical as well as technical. They don't view 'free riders' as a concern. Theirs is much more than the negligent generosity of a people who've always had enough to eat. They know from experience that it costs more to collect from free riders than it's worth.''

Still, as his father had put it on a rare occasion when he'd had too much to drink, socialism at its unclean root was no more than the politics of envy, collectively expressed resentment of achievement. A century of the oppressive poverty it always caused hadn't prepared them to appreciate what they were being given here. It even caused a few to question it.

''If the tables were turned,'' he told the doctor, ''there are plenty of us capable of resenting free riders. And precedents to show we're willing to waste resources trying to do something about it.''

''And it is these individuals who worry most about survival here. How long, they ask, can this suspicious generosity last? Why don't the Elders do what any right-thinking human would in their place? Their education hasn't prepared them to look for what you call the 'bottom line,' the ethical aspect of any economic situation.''

''And what might that be?''

''To us, ethics is more than a conflicting laundry list of free-floating rights and arbitrary wrongs. It's a discipline which asks—and in a healthy culture tries to answer—the question, 'What is the good?' ''

''Well, you're the doctor, Doctor. what is the good?''

''Self-ownership, self-responsibility, whatever you wish, provided it doesn't interfere with someone else's notion of the good. This is why the Elders never worry about free riders. When someone installs and pays for a streetlight, the benefit he seeks, if he's rational, is the light itself.''

''Sounds vaguely Masonic. As opposed to what?''

''As opposed to the dubious satisfaction of denying it to those who don't pay but may incidentally benefit. Didn't one of your own thinkers, Robert LeFevre, observe that an ethical person will blacken a portion of his light so it won't spill into the window of an unwilling beneficiary?''

Danny laughed. He seemed to be doing a lot of that lately. ''It's true that nobody in our group understands why we're being helped.''

''You find the Elders' generosity perplexing?''

''You could say that.''

''You've never observed that it is capitalist society, rather than the workers' paradise, which gives away matches, food, soap, and other commodities? The catch, if you can call it that, is that a producer advertises on the matchbook or may be handing out samples trying to get you to buy more.''

''And what's the catch on 5023 Eris?''

''Mr. Thoggosh is probably trying to think of one right now. Of course you have loaned him your spaceships. . . .''

''It's a point in our favor.'' Danny knew, however, that his father was reluctant to continue depending on the charity of strangers. Despite his socialist background, he tended, in character and principle, to value self-sufficiency and independence. Maybe he'd acquired this antisocialist trait during his training and experience as a pilot. Maybe it was just that somehow the American spirit had survived in him. In any case, the Elders' philosophy regarding the ''Forge of Adversity'' had been hovering constantly at the back of the general's mind. Danny tried to explain that to Dlee Raftan Saon.

''It seems to me they contradict what they claim to believe in. I've never been sure how much is metaphorical and—I mean, does their philosophy describe reality as they conceive it, or does it prescribe action?''

The physician considered. ''What makes you feel vulnerable is that your education led you to expect social Darwinists to be less considerate of the needs of others, although another of your philosophers, Charles Curley, defined capitalism as encouraging survival of the most helpful.''

"I'm just afraid their ideals won't let them deprive us of a chance to overcome our difficulties and transcend ourselves.''

"So that, from a kindness you feel is misplaced, the Elders may deny you further help at any time, leaving you to be tested on the Forge and perish.''

"Something like that. Don't think I'd be good at perishing gracefully.''

"Therefore, in your view as well as your father's, survival depends on seeing to your own needs as completely and as soon as possible.''

"At least these guns my dad didn't want to bring are good for something.''

"Danny, in an ethical society, no one is ever *placed* upon the Forge of Adversity. We stand upon it every instant of our lives. The greatest point in your favor is that you are here, doing what you're doing.''

"Hunting?''

"Those who make a habit of free rides do not survive in the long run.''

"I don't know, Raftan. Tax collectors have been around a long time.''

"They strive like any parasite. Still, we attach different meaning to the phrase 'long run.' You speak of hundreds of years, I of millions. Tax collectors didn't survive in our civilization. The two, tax collectors and civilization, cannot coexist—*watch out!*''

Without further warning, a gray-brown blur of feral tusks and bristles crashed from the underbrush and hurled itself in their direction. Danny had a fleeting impression of a flat black snout and amber eyes insane with rage. Lost in the moment, he clamped his gun in both hands the way his father had taught him and basic training hadn't. His right hand held the rounded rubber grip; his left hand held the right. Left arm bent, elbow pointing downward, he tipped his head as if his right arm, stiff and straight before him, were a rifle stock, and kept both eyes open.

The pig was a growing, fuzzy blob, the sharply focused orange insert of the front sight his entire world. He pulled the trigger. The chrome-frosted hammer rose and fell. The short-barreled S & W roared and bucked. He neither heard nor felt it. A ball of blue flame at the muzzle lit the woods for yards around. Danny didn't see it. All he knew was that the big silver slug had plowed a furrow in the leaves behind his target. The wild pig kept coming, straight for his legs the way they'd said it would.

He fired again, to no visible effect, then leaped at the lowest branch of a nearby tree he hadn't consciously realized was there. Scrambling until he straddled the limb, he saw the animal below him shaking itself as if it had crashed headlong into the trunk. He regretted missing that.

Aiming carefully with one hand as his other held him steady in the tree, he shot the pig between the shoulder blades. This time he felt the impact of the .44 magnum in his palm and saw the muzzle bloom with fire, although he couldn't remember hearing the report afterward. The pig went down as if a safe had been dropped on it and didn't even quiver afterward.

"Congratulations, my boy!" From the branch above him, he heard the voice of Dlee Raftan Saon. He turned his head and saw the physician clinging upside down to the tree with four of his limbs. "Low gravity's a wonderful thing, isn't it?" the insect being laughed. "You've shot a razorback sow, much hardier and more tenacious than the boar."

"Tell me about it!" Danny grinned. "Tonight *I'm* bringing home the bacon!"

XX
Swords and Plowshares

Rosalind shot another wild sow before nightfall with a single well-placed bullet to the lungs as it charged an empty jacket Owen tossed in its path. They would eat well over the next few days.

Veteran human hunters, returning as empty handed as their scorpionoid brethren, were delighted with the pair of freshly blooded novices. The pigs were field-dressed on the spot, slit from crotch to breastbone, the breastbone split, and the insides—except for the liver and heart—left for carrion eaters. Danny, stained and sticky to the elbows with his part of the task, shouldered one end of the pole his pig was tied to and grinned every step of the way back to the camp until his jaws hurt. Now he knew why some men in the nineteenth and twentieth centuries had become professionals at this "sport." He wanted to go out again tomorrow.

"Funny," Rosalind told him as she strode beside him carrying the organ meat in a plastic bag she'd brought for the purpose, "I don't feel the way I always thought I was supposed to about killing an animal. Not sad or guilty." She gave her head a toss in the direction of Alvarez and Betal, who'd demanded the honor of carrying her trophy home. "Instead, I feel like singing."

"And why not, dear colleague," Dlee Raftan Saon called to her over what would have been his shoulder if he'd had shoulders, "it's what three billion years of evolution have prepared you for!"

Rosalind smiled and curtsied to the other doctor, her service pistol incongruous on her hip. Hooray for evolution, Danny found himself thinking, and for the wild frontier. Their expedition had been colonial in concept, its members undesirables, embarrassing presences, outcasts, exiles. They'd been ordered to make a permanent home for themselves among the asteroids. Whatever they discovered they were stuck with; no resupply was planned for the foreseeable future because the Earth had no more ships. There had always been vague talk of a new fleet, but no resources. The present effort was expected to return the investment it represented to America's failing economy, in part by becoming self-sufficient as quickly possible. Well, they'd made another good start today—perhaps their first.

Something concealed in the gathering darkness hooted at him, making him jump and reminding him that he was still an amateur at this wild frontier business. He shook his head. What had he been thinking about? Oh yes. Nobody had talked about it; nobody had needed to. Their leaders hadn't wanted to mention it, and those ordered to go hadn't wanted to hear it. But if things didn't pan out, the ASSR was rid of a lot of misfits. Later—much later—if they proved successful, new ships might be built to relieve the first arrivals. Earth had plenty of unwanted characters to be sent hundreds of millions of kilometers away. Now that Danny had discovered that he could feed himself and his friends, none of these considerations seemed as grim—or even important—as they had before. He had learned a lesson socialism never dared teach: the joy of individual independence.

The hunting party hadn't strayed far into the forest, so it wasn't long before they reached camp again. It looked much as it had from the beginning. In the flickering firelight even the new tents fooled the eye for a moment, standing beside the offloaded passenger modules in place of the shuttles.

There was no lack of shoulders to relieve Danny, Betal,

Alvarez, and Jones of their burdens. Despite the absence of the general, Ortiz, Sebastiano, and their minimal crews, the camp seemed crowded. In addition to the American expeditionaries, temporarily commanded by Empleado, Mr. Thoggosh was present, in the complete flesh, shell and everything, to greet them this time, along with his assistant, Aelbraugh Pritsch. One reason, perhaps, that the camp seemed crowded was that Scutigera, who took up a lot of room all by himself, had come with them.

"Auspicious beginnings," the great centipede declared. "Congratulations. I shouldn't have thought your weapons adequate to the task."

Danny grinned up at the enormous being who, for once, wasn't making him feel like the next dinner course. "There's little, sir, in this or any other world that a .44 magnum isn't adequate for."

He didn't mention that it had taken him three shots to get the job done, or that Rosalind had killed her pig with a single, less powerful .41x22. He was about to speak of her when he was shouldered aside by Andre Valerian, one of the agricultural specialists included in all three shuttle crew complements. Danny was fairly certain the Russian was what he appeared to be, and not just another KGB agent traveling incognito. With him was Captain Guillermo, a soil geologist, and Major Ortega y Pena, another scientific type—a botanist whom everyone referred to (behind his back) as "Pinhead."

"Corporal Owen!"

The machinist ducked out from the crowd of well-wishers and welcomers to address the major. "You rang?"

"Take a look at this." Ortega held out a metallic object, indistinct in the darkness. "How do you explain it?"

"I don't know, Major. It would help if I could see it better." Before the indignant botanist could reply, Eichra Oren was beside the corporal, shining a powerful light down at the object in Owen's broad hand. Sam was at the Antarctican's knee and Pulaski was within an arm's length.

It took a moment before Danny realized that the "flashlight" was the plasma pistol, a multipurpose tool with which Eichra Oren had held off one of Empleado's thugs after they'd first arrived on the asteroid. "Okay, that's the nose-piece of the plow blade I made for you aggie people, and it's sheared off. Pretty neat trick, Pin—I mean, Major. It's graphitic tool steel, hardened to sixty-five on the Rockwell 'C' scale. How'd it happen?"

Ortega sniffed. "I expected you to tell me, Corporal."

Owen ran his fingers through his black, bushy beard and hair. He'd neither shaved nor had a haircut in months and often looked like a wildman to his fellow humans. God knew, Danny thought, what he looked like to the aliens. The lieutenant often thought of him as the world's biggest hobbit. "Gee, Maje, I expected to win the state lottery someday, too, but it never happened. I got sent here, instead. Life's full of disappointments, isn't it? Let's go sit by the fire and talk. You used the winch with this?"

The group adjourned to the center of the camp where logs had been laid as seats around what had become a permanent firepit. Several people took charge of the pigs. There were compartments within the tent walls in which food never spoiled, even though it remained at ambient temperature and was subjected to no detectable radiation.

The agricultural experts had started a little garden under a sheet-plastic greenhouse. Among the expedition's most important supplies were fast-growing high-yield seeds of various kinds. Twentieth-century experience with Lunar soil samples had led this mission's planners to expect fast growth and high yield in uneroded carbonaceous chondrite despite the fact that less sunlight was available beyond the orbit of Mars. Before taking off on a hunting expedition of his own, General Gutierrez had decided it was time to put both experts and supplies to their intended use.

At Ortega's order, some of the personnel had begun laying out a plot next to the encampment. Various individuals from the nautiloid establishment had come from time to time to observe the quaint agricultural practices of the barbarians. Thanks to a nearby stream and the soft rains that fell almost every night, there was no lack of water. A shallow ditch had been scraped to divert a little water to the garden. Everyone had expected that the soft, crumbly carbonaceous chondrite soil would work easily. If the Lunar soil experiments were any guide, all one had to do was shove the seeds into the ground, sprinkle on some water, and jump back out of the way.

The experts had assured everyone that, despite the canopy, there was more than enough light to grow crops. All one had to do, if unconvinced, was look at the jungle growing all around them. Danny had, and began to wonder why it was necessary to plant their own crops when more food than they could ever use seemed to be hanging wild on every tree and bush. Owen had spoken of little else all the way back to camp, wondering aloud if the local equivalent of tomatoes, garlic, mustard, and onions they'd already discovered would make suitable barbecue sauce for pork. He'd spoken with Raftan, Tl*m*nch*l, and Dr*f*rst*v about vinegar and brown sugar. Danny hadn't had the heart to remind the corporal that at any moment they might be cut off from all this largesse, especially since Marna, who outranked him, had joined the conversation, arguing for sweet-and-sour instead of barbecue.

However, if everything else went as it should, they would soon have their own food supply, and if somebody didn't happen to like broccoli, cauliflower, or brussels sprouts, it was too bad. The trouble was, Danny grinned with ironic appreciation, he'd never liked broccoli, cauliflower, or brussels sprouts himself. On the other hand, he thought, when since landing on this asteroid, had anything gone as it should? This was yet another thought, he realized, which, like the political opinions he shared with his father, was best kept to himself.

Owen had asked Ortega, ''You used the winch with this?''

The botanist bobbed his head as if he were the corporal

and Owen the major. "As you instructed." Since the expedition was shorter on available labor than land, they'd adopted a semimechanized plan to make their furrows radial instead of parallel, each terminating at a common point. There, Owen had set up a powerful electric motor and steel cable to drag the plowshare through the dirt from the far ends of the furrows to the center.

"It appears that the topsoil in the chosen location is only centimeters deep," Valerian told the machinist while glaring at the soil geologist, Guillermo. "Almost immediately our rig hit impermeable bedrock—we couldn't stop the motor in time—destroying the blade."

Running a thumb over the jagged edge, Owen raised his eyebrows. "And what about the spare blade I made you?"

A long-suffering Guillermo polished his glasses and sighed, "I'm afraid this *is* the spare blade, Corporal."

"Well," replied the machinist, "before we left to go hunting, I was working on a third blade, cobbled together from carbide-edged titanium alloy, but I'd like to see this bedrock of yours before I finish it. I can't guarantee that it won't meet the same fate."

"I can guarantee that it will," declared a familiar voice. They turned to watch Mr. Thoggosh drag himself into the firelight. Covered in plastic that kept his body moist, the mollusc glistened. "It's the same problem I've been having and the reason I came to visit you tonight. You may wonder why none of us is amused at your mishap. I observed what you would-be farmers went through with sympathy. You see, I've been making—rather the scientists and technicians in my employ have—a series of bewildering discoveries about this troublesome asteroid. If you'll accompany me to the place your agricultural implement failed, I'll tell you about some of them."

"I just suggested that," Owen told Mr. Thoggosh. "Got a flashlight?"

He was answered by a burst of blue-green brightness and a loud, hollow-sounding hiss. Behind Mr. Thoggosh, Llessure

Knarrfic, looking, as she always did, like a six-foot-tall rubber flower, held one of the expedition's Coleman lanterns. "Excellent, Lieutenant," the plant-being declared to Marna, who stood beside her blowing on a burnt-out survival match. "It has a robust flavor I've never experienced with artificial light before."

Marna grinned and shook her head. Several people turned to listen.

"I thought you were supposed to be a carnivorous plant," objected Danny, who'd been content to watch until now. "That's what Raftan told me, anyway. He said your people hunt—just like we do."

"That's what I told him," the insect physician confirmed, his faceted eyes glittering in the lamplight.

The enormous flower swiveled her blossomlike face to look at him. "Just because I'm a vegetable, did you think I have to be a vegetarian? That's the animal thinking process. Of course we hunt, young person. But we're also photosynthetic, like any proper org—er, plant life. By the way, Corporal, I agree with Lee: sweet-and-sour sounds ever so much better than this bar-bee-queue you suggested. Shall I kill a pig of my own? I'm looking forward to the feast. Now, are we going to see this tragic furrow of yours, or not?"

Owen laughed and led the way. A rather large, slow procession wound between two of the tents in the direction of the stream, its pace set by Mr. Thoggosh who didn't have the option of buoyant levitation that he enjoyed in his own quarters. As he drew himself along with his tentacles, dragging his shell behind him, he continued his explanation.

"I already knew there was something strange about this planetoid's composition," Mr. Thoggosh told them. "I'd have been surprised had it proved otherwise. I was attracted to this asteroid in the first place because it had no equivalent in any other parallel universe."

They found the furrow when Demene Wise, still on crutches, stumbled in it. Rosalind rushed forward to get him on his feet again. The man, another former KGB ruffian, even managed a self-deprecating laugh, something he'd have been incapable of only days before. Whatever difficulties the asteroid presented, Danny thought, being here seemed to be good for some people.

"It persists in destroying my custom-designed drilling equipment at various sites deep in what you call the super-kudzu forest. Understand we're speaking of nuclear plasma bolides, not tool steel. Now I've learned, with the help of your father and his associates, Lieutenant Gutierrez, that it also renders the asteroid opaque to neutrino scanning."

"What?" Several people gasped the word at once. Insects began to be attracted to the light and somewhere deep in the forest a night bird made a gobbling noise, mocking them.

"Indeed," the nautiloid replied, "and this, as we all know, is quite impossible—unless 5023 Eris were as dense as a collapsed star."

Owen was down on one knee in the furrow, brushing soil away from the infamous bedrock with the aid of Llessure Knarrfic's lamplight. Danny leaned over and watched as the machinist ran his short, blunt fingers over a surface that looked to the lieutenant like the dried peel of an orange, highly magnified. He wasn't disturbed to feel the tips of Scutigera's long, sensitive, tapering antennae slide past his neck like armor-covered snakes as he craned for a look at the ground below.

Owen had other ideas. "Petrified dinosaur hide," he declared. "But the whole asteroid can't consist of material as dense as you say, Mr. Thoggosh. Its gravity would exceed that of Earth."

"I'm sure," Mr. Thoggosh replied, "the astronomical-minded among you have followed much the same line of thought, Corporal. It can lead to one conclusion only, not one I like much, but consistent with what we know. This asteroid's impermeable surface—"

Danny interrupted. "Is nothing more than a hollow shell!" His words seemed to die as soon as they were spoken, absorbed by the nearby woods. A breeze stirred its leaves before Mr. Thoggosh spoke again.

"Quite right. And to account for the low gravity, it has to be a thin shell, at that. As fantastic as it seems, 5023 Eris appears to be—"

"A giant spaceship!" Toya almost screamed the words that caused another round of gasps among her fellow humans.

"Go to the head of the class, my dear. The Predecessors *constructed* 5023 Eris, dwarfing any of their previous artifacts."

XXI
Hinges of Hell

"More like a space station than a spaceship. No exhaust ports, no nozzles, no engines."

Horatio Gutierrez strode from the forest margin where he'd been all but invisible in the darkness. Looking worn and tired to his son, he stepped into the blue-white circle of the hissing Coleman. Behind him loomed the shadowy forms of Sebastiano and Ortiz.

"As far as we can tell, anyway." He glanced at the small crowd gathered about the furrow. "What's in the hole—and why do I have a feeling you haven't all turned out to welcome homecoming spacemen?"

"Dear me!" Aelbraugh Pritsch squawked. "Back already! If you'd let me know, General, I might have arranged transportation for you and your—"

"It was a nice evening for a walk," Gutierrez grinned wearily. "We left our ships upstairs"—he lifted a thumb—"parked on the outer surface ready to be lowered. The rest of our crews stayed behind in your area to have dinner on Mr. Thoggosh. You can arrange transport for them, if you like. Some of them may not be walking too well before long.''

Aelbraugh Pritsch glanced at his employer for confirmation and received it via implant. ''I'll do that, General, and send this electrostat back for Mr. Thoggosh. Would anyone care to return with me now?''

Scutigera, too large for any flying machine available, excused himself anyway, saying he'd intended to go back to his quarters before now. Llessure Knarrfic and the scorpionoid guards accepted the offer of a ride. Sam, too, declared that he had a personal errand and disappeared into the woods.

Wise had begun to weave on his crutches. Sweat trickled down the side of his neck although the night was cool. Rosalind ordered him to bed and took him that way under escort.

Marna declared that she wanted a look at the shuttles' life-support systems before they were powered down. Alvarez volunteered to go along as an extra pair of hands, but not before he gave Betal and Jones detailed instruction in preparing the wild pigs for the meal he planned tomorrow.

Owen, conferring with Ortega and Valerian, decided there wasn't any point in repeating the plow experiment until Guillermo found an area nearby where the soil lay deeper over whatever 5023 Eris was made of. Ortega and Valerian said good night. Guillermo stayed to continue the discussion. The machinist ambled off to put his winch away.

Danny noticed that Empleado wasn't around anymore, having vanished without a word, which seemed appropriate for the KGB.

Ortiz and Sebastiano excused themselves to try out the showers with which the tents had come equipped and, before retiring, check on members of their crews who hadn't gone on the capture mission. Neither was the original captain of his spacecraft, and each took his new responsibility seriously.

Danny saw that his father needed rest, too, but knew he wouldn't take it until his own responsibilities were discharged.

That included discussing Mr. Thoggosh's new information, since it was to this that he steered the conversation as he led the handful who remained to the tent that was still lighted.

"Also, if it's a Predecessor ship, why is it here in orbit around the Sun?" He went to a table, poured coffee, and found a chair. Eichra Oren, Pulaski, Guillermo, Dlee Raftan Saon, and Danny followed his example. "Why didn't it disappear a long time ago to wherever they went?"

Mr. Thoggosh abandoned a final pretense of helplessness out of water since he couldn't drag himself across the tent floor without rumpling the fabric. Looking like a misshapen spider, he took advantage of the low gravity to rise to the tips of his tentacles and step delicately into the center of the room, where he settled.

"We've no significant argument, sir—"

"Although," Raftan interjected, "I might ask the general where the exhaust ports or rocket nozzles of one of his culture's nineteenth-century Yankee clipper ships were to be found."

"We agree the place is artificial," Mr. Thoggosh went on. "Knowing as little as we do of the Predecessors' impressive accomplishments, who's to say there aren't any engines?"

Eichra Oren nodded, looking to Pulaski for support, perhaps because she was the closest thing they had to an archaeologist. "Given their technology, they might turn out to be the size of a walnut."

Raftan agreed. "Mr. Thoggosh, I suspect that your assistant, were he here, might hold that since 5023 Eris floats freely in space, circling a sun rather than a planet or moon, it must be a spaceship—"

"I must be getting tired," the general interrupted. "You've lost me."

Mr. Thoggosh lifted a resigned limb. "In this context, the distinction between a space station and a spaceship is pointless. We argue to no purpose, as is often the case when fresh facts fail to present themselves, and I, too, am a trifle fatigued." He glanced—wistfully, Danny thought—at the coffeepot. "To any extent I care, I hope it's the latter. The idea of a spaceship the size of a world, even a small world, rather strikes my fancy."

"And," Eichra Oren suggested, "machinery powerful enough to move a world—even a small world like this—would be extremely valuable."

Mr. Thoggosh shrugged. "I hope it isn't a defective spaceship."

"What?" That from several present.

"What if, at the last moment, it was abandoned as flawed?"

Raftan nodded. "It betrays every manifestation of abandonment, even to having acquired an outer coating of natural asteroidal material."

"Not substantial enough to suit my ag people." Gutierrez paused as if in thought, then grimaced with resignation and asked his son for a cigarette.

Danny leaned toward his father to light it, then lit one of his own. "Sir, all this carbonaceous chondrite might be meant to disguise the true nature of 5023 Eris from casual observers."

His father agreed. "It would also be cheap protection from radiation and meteorites, except that this place doesn't seem to need it."

"Or it might be the inevitable effect of ages spent orbiting among real asteroids," Mr. Thoggosh argued, "since they're seventy percent carbonaceous chondrite. The inference can be made either way. It's just another question no one knows the answer to."

"With no way of finding out," Danny added.

"On the contrary, Lieutenant. Eichra Oren, show them what we brought. They're what you'd call 'hard copy' from the neutrino scan. I'd like to have your experts, in addition to those among my party, examine them."

The Antarctican unrolled a sheaf of what appeared to be photographs, printed on some sort of heavy white plastic rather than paper. In them, the asteroid occupied the entire frame. The canopy was invisible, as was the jungle. The Elders' buildings—and in one picture features of the human camp—seemed transparent, ghostlike. The asteroidal layering, whatever its origin and purpose, formed a kind of second skin underneath which the impermeable core of 5023 Eris lay flawless and unbroken. The humans took turns peering at the photos, searching for a clue to the mysteries the asteroid continued to generate.

"Well, here's a small apparent flaw." It was Guillermo, pointing to a section of the asteroid's otherwise armored hull. Four feet away, Danny couldn't see the feature he referred to. Mr. Thoggosh slid forward.

"I see what you mean. If you'll excuse me . . ."

Guillermo backed away, watching. The nautiloid placed a slender tentacle-tip on the map where the captain's finger had been. The image on the plastic sheet swelled and acquired more detail. "I quite agree, Captain. It might be a small meteor crater, but there should be a great many more of them if it is. It looks to me as if it might well turn out, upon examination, to be a large, well-buried door. Or perhaps that's only wishful thinking on my part. What do you say, General?"

Gutierrez leaned over the map, then compared it with several of the other documents. "Looks like it's about five meters below the natural carbonaceous chondrite surface— and, wouldn't you know it, almost on the opposite side of the asteroid from here."

"So it is," replied Mr. Thoggosh, beginning to sound excited. "Now to rush my weary and exasperated drilling crews to the site. Here at last is something they can get their teeth into. Will you be joining us, sir? I'll call for another electrostat."

Gutierrez sighed. "Call for two. I'll bring Danny along as my aide. Our physician and machinist should come." He looked up at Toya, as usual of late standing as close as she could to Eichra Oren. "Also our resident paleontologist.

And I suppose I'd better invite Arthur and Sergeant Jones or there'll be hell to pay.'' He turned to Guillermo. ''Hector, in the absence of the late Dr. Kamanov, you're our chief geologist. Go round up whatever you need, notify the people I just named, those who aren't here already, and get back here five minutes ago.''

Guillermo grinned. ''Yes, sir!''

''General, you're in need of sleep. It will take hours to dig that far. Rest and join us later.'' There was concern in Mr. Thoggosh's voice.

Gutierrez stood up straight and stretched. ''Thanks, Mr. Thoggosh, I'll sleep in the aerocraft. It couldn't keep me awake if it flew around this world upside down and backwards!''

For once, to everyone's amazement, everything worked.

After placing Sebastiano in charge of the camp, the general got his much-needed in-flight nap and more opportunity to rest once they'd arrived at the broad green meadow on the day side of 5023 Eris corresponding to the small feature Guillermo had discovered on the neutrino map.

At Rosalind's suggestion, they'd detoured into the treetops above the nautiloid settlement to retrieve half a dozen spacesuits from the shuttles. If the asteroid were hollow as they had come to believe, she argued, and artificial, then hundreds of million years of corrosion would long since have removed any breathable oxygen from whatever atmosphere hadn't seeped into space, molecule by molecule.

Mr. Thoggosh ordered a great pit dug, five meters deep and thirty in diameter. Looking more like recoilless artillery or giant bazookas than industrial equipment, his mining machinery, which had proved useless against the obstinate material of the asteroid itself, hissed and roared on its supporting framework amid unbearable brilliance, clearing soft soil off the impenetrable substrate in a matter of minutes, almost vaporizing it and somehow compressing it into glassy bricks which were used to support the sloping sides of the excavation.

In due course, they found a huge triangular hatch with rounded sides and corners, 'trochoidal' someone called it, ten meters on a side. After their earlier trouble, it wasn't even locked. Despite its being a meter thick and composed of the same material as the rest of 5023 Eris, it lifted on counterbalancing pivots. An unlit chamber of unknown dimension and contents awaited. Not knowing what to expect, nervous explorers, human and otherwise, suited up and prepared to descend into the cavernous interior.

The initial party consisted of Gutierrez and his son, Owen, Rosalind, Guillermo, and Eichra Oren in a borrowed NASA suit. Mr. Thoggosh had ordered light, transparent gear made to fit the humans (and a canine suit, as well). The next explorers would be more comfortable, but no one wanted to wait until new equipment was available. Tl*m*nch*l, two others of his species, and Nannel Rab, the spiderlike chief project engineer, completed the group. Given the density of the surface material, communication with the those remaining behind would have to be by wire, trailed behind them. Several individuals, not just humans, pointed out the similarity between this situation and that of old-time "hard hat" deep-sea divers.

Representing Mr. Thoggosh, Eichra Oren was the first to duck beneath the uptilted corner and drop a full ten meters to the floor of the triangular chamber. One by one, he was followed by the others, the giant spider squeezing through last. Eichra Oren popped up again to deliver a distressing report to Mr. Thoggosh and Sam (who was already upset at being left behind) while hanging on the edge by his fingers.

"It's an idiot-proof airlock," he told them, pushing a gloved thumb over his shoulder toward the point beyond the massive pivot where the large counterbalancing end of the triangular hatch tilted downward. "And guess who the idiots are. The next door below swings into this chamber, and right now it's blocked by this one. It won't move a centimeter until this hatch is closed and out of the way."

"Ingenious," his employer answered. "Which means that if you go on, we'll lose contact with you."

Gutierrez joined Eichra Oren. Hanging there, the would-be explorers looked like oddly dressed swimmers chatting with poolside friends. "That's about the size of it. Corporal Owen says this slab fits to a ten-thousandth. I don't know if he meant millimeters or inches, but it'll shear any wire we try to leave behind."

"Or jam on it," Sam offered, "and we'll never get you out."

Eichra Oren grinned inside his visor. "There's a cheerful thought. I don't see that we have any choice about it, though. We're as well prepared as it's possible to be, and the sooner we get on with it, the better. Watch your fingers when the lid comes down."

With that, he let go of the edge. The general dropped beside him. They strode across the chamber to their waiting comrades. Danny and Corporal Owen stretched themselves and leaped to give the rear edge of the hatch cover a shove. It would be meters beyond their reach once it was back in place, but the single push was all it needed. It pivoted and settled with a thump, plunging them all into darkness.

Several light beams sprang into existence. With the interfering upper hatch out of the way, the inner hatch swung aside as if it had been made of balsa wood and had been used the day before instead of millions, perhaps billions of years ago.

XXII
Looking for Pellucidar

"Holy shit—" The voice was Danny's. Sheepish at his own outburst, he added, "Batman."

It would have been pitch black without their helmet lights and the hand-held lamps the scorpionoids had brought. In the yellow beams they saw that they'd entered a half-sphere forty meters in diameter. The hatch they'd come through was set in the flat side. The curved surface was broken every few meters by an open trochoidal tunnel-mouth, giving the impression that they hung suspended over an enormous sieve.

They found themselves half swimming in the chamber, the gravity they'd come to feel as normal no longer pulling. It was an indication of the density of the shell they'd penetrated, how much it contributed to the mass of 5023 Eris. In spite of that, it appeared that the asteroid wasn't hollow like a basketball as they'd imagined. Each of them grimly visualized thousands upon thousands of kilometers of dark, twisted passageways worm-riddling what they still thought of as a natural body despite the fact, Danny realized, that it was as artificial as the battered ASF-issue Seiko on his wrist.

It was cold, just above zero Celsius. Nannel Rab and the scorpionoids (it amused Danny that they sounded like a rock group) carried instruments to sniff the contents of the chamber. They reported that it consisted mostly of vacuum—one millibar, about the same atmospheric pressure as Mars, a thousandth of Earth normal—but with traces of nitrogen, oxygen, carbon dioxide, hydrocarbons and, intriguingly, fluorocarbon.

Pulaski peering over his shoulder, Owen examined the walls, constructed, or at least lined, with a seamless plastic, ribbed for traction. A scratch with the Czech army knife he always carried showed that it was almost as indestructible as the surface. Others peered into each of the tunnels without entering any, shining lamps down them until vision was obstructed by a curve or the light was absorbed by distance. Gutierrez and Eichra Oren conferred about the order of march and chose the entrance nearest the center.

They made an impressive party: seven humans in bulky suits who might appear frightening to a nonhuman race, three outsized lobsters and a huge red and black spider in almost invisible outer skins. Despite every sign that the place had been deserted for thousands of millennia, no one had tried to talk them out of arming themselves to whatever their respective species used for teeth; 5023 Eris had already presented them with too many surprises.

"We ought to leave some kind of markings as we go," Guillermo observed, "like bread crumbs or Huck Finn's ball of twine."

"Tom Sawyer," Owen corrected, although no one could remember whether he or the geologist was right.

Eichra Oren chuckled. "Sam wouldn't let me come without these." He extracted a package, took something out, and flattened it against the wall nearest the chosen tunnel. When he took his hand away, he'd left a glowing spot. "Powered by background radiation. They should last several centuries."

"I wish you hadn't said that." Through the thickness of Tl*m*nch*l's suit, Danny heard the speech sounds he made, like an old manual typewriter. "I didn't know I was claustrophobic until now. Going down that tunnel will be like crawling through the intestines of some unspeakable giant."

"I wish you hadn't said *that*!" Pulaski told the scorpionoid.

At last there was no more reason to put it off. The general led the way, followed by Danny, Nannel Rab, and Eichra Oren. Tl*m*nch*l, his comrades, Guillermo, and Owen were the rear guard. Rosalind and Toya were sandwiched between, fear of the unknown prompting an unconscious return to chivalry. Danny noticed that both women gravitated toward Eichra Oren when the going was especially scary. It gave the man a look of distinct pain, visible even through his helmet. At the same time, mutual repulsion seemed to be at work between the women. It was almost as interesting as the physics of the asteroid itself.

The corridor they entered, like those they'd rejected, was built low and wide for the original occupants, who'd been neither humanoid nor nautiloid. Nannel Rab, the real giant among them, had a difficult time, but refused, given a chance, to return to the surface. After the first curve, one hundred meters from the entrance, the path branched at a spherical junction. They had to choose from a dozen alternatives. Eichra Oren marked the tunnel they'd come from. Guteirrez chose another that seemed to lead toward the asteroid's center. The Antarctican slapped a glowing patch beside it.

Geometry dictated, Guillermo maintained, that it wasn't possible for all the tunnels to branch this way. As they made their way deeper, the atmosphere thickened, the temperature rose, and, after several junctions had proven Guillermo wrong, they began to see what appeared to be pooled remnants of the same liquid fluorocarbon that filled Mr. Thoggosh's office. To some of the explorers, that meant the previous occupants had been marine creatures.

"Hold on," Gutierrez argued, "is there any indication the Predecessors needed fluorocarbons to deal with non-marine sapients?"

Pulaski shook her head, the gesture lost until she spoke. "There's no indication that other sapients even existed when the Predecessors did."

"Score a point for the ship theory," the general declared,

picking his way around a large puddle clinging to the wall they'd arbitrarily decided was the floor. "This stuff, if it filled the whole place, would transfer momentum nicely, increasing the passengers' tolerance for acceleration."

"It might just have been a way of transferring garbage," Nannel Rab suggested. "It wouldn't be the first open sewer system I've heard of in so-called civilized realms. Who can outguess another species?"

Owen grunted. "Especially one that's been extinct a billion years."

"Whatever its purpose," Rosalind stated, leaning over an instrument the giant spider carried, "over the time it's been here, it's lost its oxygen and turned foul. This stuff has a nasty color. I'm glad we can't smell it."

According to Guillermo and Nannel Rab, the pools of liquid shouldn't have grown larger and more frequent as they burrowed deeper. They also grew uglier in color and consistency, although the main ingredient remained a fluorocarbon similar to one they were familiar with. As they groped from one branch to another, they never knew what to expect. In some places the remaining chemical "atmosphere" (despite Nannel Rab's suggestion, that was what they continued to believe it was) had deteriorated until it was opaque.

"Holy mother of God!" Gutierrez was the first to come across a chamber filled with the stuff. Its condition had awakened a childhood verbal reflex.

"What is it?" several voices responded at once.

"You have to see this to believe it," he told them in disgust, "and we don't have any choice about wading through it."

By that time, Danny had caught up to his father and saw what he was talking about. The once-liquid contents of the chamber had jelled into a mass into which Gutierrez had stumbled. He'd managed to back out, but it covered his suit in putrescent-looking brown slime marbled with streaks of black. Danny switched his transmitter off and risked touching his visor to his father's. "Dad, you've been spending too much time with the KGB."

His father chuckled. "I've been in deep shit before, but—"

"General!" Rosalind pushed past Danny, her helmet hiding an expression of disgust that her tone betrayed. "I wanted to warn you about removing any part of your suit before its exterior is sterilized. There may be dangerous microbes here that have been multiplying and mutating for eons."

Gutierrez nodded. "Understood, Doctor. That goes for everybody. I want individual confirmation that you heard it, starting with you, Lieutenant."

"Yes, sir. What do we do, scrub down with peroxide?"

"We'll leave that to Rosalind. For now, we all have to slog through this gunk, and I want her warning understood. Hector? Corporal Owen?"

One by one they replied, including the nonhumans. Hoping this chamber wasn't the start of a whole asteroid filled with filth the consistency of Vaseline, Danny held his breath and took the plunge. Crossing that chamber was the most revolting task he'd ever faced, but his worst fear failed to be realized. After twenty meters of it, he broke through, not into thin air, but into clear, healthy-looking fluorocarbon which washed the slime from his suit. They waited and the rest of the party soon emerged.

Once past that unpleasant chamber, the corridors widened as if intended by the original occupants to be gathering spots. Here the ancient ship or station appeared even better preserved. To their astonishment the walls glowed with a light like that of the contrastingly colored adhesive spots Eichra Oren still left behind them.

"I guess," the general declared, "this is what we came to see."

They began by exploring rooms branching off from the corridors. All had heavy, tight-fitting triangular doors without anything like a lock. Some were clearly residential. Others might have been offices, laboratories, physical plant control rooms, infirmaries, or eating places.

What might have been a sanitary facility they tentatively identified merely by the endless ranks of grotesquely shaped low-standing ceramic objects bolted to its floor. If that was what they were, Danny wasn't sure he ever wanted to meet the creatures they'd been designed for. On the other hand, they could have been the equivalent of slot machines.

And what were they to make of a domed chamber in which there stood a construct one hundred meters tall which called to mind a great radio telescope or directional antenna connected at its base to a lighthouse, complete with a glassed-in booth at the top, but which pointed nowhere but a blank wall of solid, plastic-covered metal?

Another find was even more peculiar. The room was the size of a football stadium. Its ceiling, however, was only a little over a meter high and they had to stoop to explore it. It was filled with precise rows of featureless solid metal cubes half a meter on a side, capable of sliding easily across a floor that seemed to Danny like greased Teflon—although it provided perfect traction for their booted feet. Any cube, once moved and released, glided sedately back into its place, others getting out of its way if necessary before resuming their own positions.

It was a frustrating experience. What was the purpose of the dozens of gimballed, dust-filled rooms they discovered, drum shapes lying on their sides, resembling a geologist's rock tumbler? (For all the explorers knew, they might have been car washes or torture chambers.) Pulaski suggested that this was how the Predecessors cleaned and polished their (hypothetical) exoskeletons. If so, how had they kept from injuring themselves? And what had the polishing medium been, long since wasted away to nothing?

The great majority of rooms and fixtures couldn't be identified that far, or even guessed at, either by the humans or the species accompanying them. "Yes, but what will future archaeologists make," Guillermo asked his companions pointedly, "of one of our rooms back on Earth, half-filled with brightly colored Ping-Pong balls?"

"Forget future archaeologists," demanded Tl*m*nch*l. "*I'd* like to know what humans do with a room half-filled with brightly colored Ping-Pong balls. Something suitably salacious, I trust."

"What sort of creature is a Ping-Pong?" Nannel Rab asked. "Poor things."

In all their explorations, the fascinated, frustrated party discovered nothing like written records. Visible technology was sophisticated enough to have made the equivalent of a library or computer unrecognizable. Few of the smaller artifacts Mr. Thoggosh collected seemed to have been left behind.

At the widest points in the passageways the walls were divided into textured areas with raised borders. To human eyes, everything about them was a burnished golden bronze. "Paintings or sculptures," Pulaski guessed, "maybe both."

"Abstracts," Rosalind agreed, "intended for senses different from ours."

Owen grinned. "I'll bet they all say 'Eat At Joe's.' " Nobody laughed; it was as good a guess as any.

"Whatever they are," Eichra Oren observed after feeling them, "they don't seem representational." He explained the tactiles Mr. Thoggosh fancied. These were rather like the Proprietor's collection at home, he said, perhaps intended to please and amuse those who passed by them in the corridors.

"General! Eichra Oren! Come look at this!"

In the center of the next "square," Nannel Rab had encountered a large representational metal statue. Struggling against the drag of the liquid atmosphere, Gutierrez hurried. "The damned thing's bronze colored," he observed, puffing inside his helmet, "like everything else."

The others were close behind. It was four meters long, three meters tall and about the same width, squatted over a broad pedestal on what might have been a traffic island in a shopping mall. There was no way of telling whether it was realistic in scale or heroic, but judging from the corridors around them—if it portrayed the sapients who had made it—it had been rendered in true-to-life proportions. "It's possible, '' one scorpionoid observed, ''that this indicates the physical nature of the Predecessors. It's consistent with the size and shape of the doorways.''

''Otherhandwise,'' Owen argued, ''a thing like this may tell us nothing.''

''Beyond something of their aesthetic preferences,'' Pulaski noted.

''Right,'' the corporal continued. ''Humans are fond of sculpture and a lot of it depicts other species. There was a famous sculpture of a seagull once in Salt Lake where the Beehive Commune later put up the statue of Geraldo Rivera. And a real good one of a moose,'' he added, ''in St. John's. And what about that Picasso thingamacallit in front of party headquarters in Chicago?''

''Or all the renderings,'' nodded the paleontologist, getting into the spirit, ''of seven-foot-tall mice in the Disneylands.''

''A month ago,'' the general answered, running a glove over the sculpture, ''I wouldn't have believed in nautiloids or hyperthyroid spiders.'' The thing depicted here was long, wide, flat, segmented, and possessed many short, jointed legs. In some ways it was like the sow bugs—''roly-polies'' —children play with. ''If this is representational, I won't have a lot more trouble believing in giant, sapient trilobites.''

For want of a better reaction, each of them in his or her own fashion shrugged and decided to move on. The ancient craft may have been strange, but it wasn't completely incomprehensible. One by one, they identified various practical installations like life support and communications, along with an impressive array of what looked like weapons systems. Although they'd yet to find the weapons themselves— or how they operated through the impenetrable barrier of the hull—it began to seem that 5023 Eris had been a battleship of some kind.

''Yeah, but the Deathstar,'' Danny muttered, ''was supposed to have been fully operational.'' He gazed down from the ''balcony'' of what they believed was a fire-control gallery, a vast, dimly lit auditorium dwarfing any opera house he'd heard of. Only their suits kept his voice from echoing.

"A good trick," his father observed, standing beside him, "since, so far, we've discovered nothing resembling any sort of engines or drive."

Danny blinked. "It was a station, then, intended to cover the Predecessors' retreat. But from what? We could find out if we activated some of these systems."

"I agree," Eichra Oren offered. He sat on a rail, his back to endless stepped ranks of consoles far below. "Our first object might be to rid the ship of these stagnant fluorocarbons. I wouldn't be surprised if fresh liquid from reservoirs deeper down began to displace those that have spoiled."

"Neither would I," replied the general. "Still, would you be willing to take your helmet off and try breathing this stuff?"

The man was about to answer, but stared instead in the direction they'd come from. The implant look, Danny thought, although they'd already confirmed that radio wouldn't carry through the structure of the asteroid and their plan to string wires to the surface had been canceled by the way the airlock worked. "It's Sam," Eichra Oren told them. "He'll be here any second."

"I am here," the dog corrected, half swimming out of the nearest corridor in a transparent suit. "Out of breath. I wanted to surprise you, but you caught me swearing at that room full of gunge back there. My message'll be surprise enough. Surprise: there's another party of human 'interlopers' —Aelbraugh Pritsch's words—threatening to arrive. Seems there's been another change of policy following the recent shift of regimes, and a small fleet, cobbled together in haste, has taken off from the Soviet Union."

"Why the hurry, Sam?" Danny asked. "It'll take them a year to get here."

"Somebody's been keeping secrets, Lieutenant," the dog replied. "They're fusion powered, constant boost. They're coming, they've announced for our benefit, to claim the

United World Soviet's share of the fruits of a 'joint cooperative mission.' The flagship, the U.S.S.R. *Lavrenti Pavlovich Beria*, has somebody onboard that Juan Sebastiano calls the Banker."

XXIII
Midnight Sun

By the time they made it to the surface, there was more news.

"Five-oh-two-three Eris, this here's ASF Fleet Admiral Dan Delacroix aboard the flagship ASSR John Reed. I wanna speak with..." The drawling voice paused as if reading from a memo. *"General Horatio Z. Gutierrez. You all copy down there?"*

"This is Gutierrez." From the excavation site he'd hurried around the little world, into the treetops over the nautiloid settlement, and out through a ribbed plastic tube connecting 5023 Eris with his ship. Innocent as yet of any newly arrived fleet, the sky held only stars twinkling down on an unending mustard plain of fused leaves. Work crews swarmed over all three vessels, preparing them for another unanticipated mission. Sam and Eichra Oren were with Gutierrez on the command deck. They still wore their suits and had been warned to seal them again while the hull was penetrated for installation of another nautiloid-designed control system. Workers moving overhead made pounding and drilling noises. The general bent the suit mike to his lips.

"I've heard of you, Admiral." What he'd heard was that Delacroix made a deceptive, dangerous enemy. Behind that cultivated Texas accent, he concealed a ruthless shrewdness honed at Harvard and Annapolis. "I don't know of any *John Reed*. I thought I had our only three spaceships. Over."

"That's what you s'posed to believe, General. The USSR ain't the only power buildin' spaceships. I'm told you got a fourth yourself, that the whole damned asteroid's artificial! Over."

My tax dollars at work, he thought—*for the KGB*. "Yes, Admiral, I've just returned from an initial survey of the interior. 5023 Eris is some kind of ancient space vessel. Over."

The man paused as if absorbing an unlikely truth. The noise conducted through the hull grew worse. Added to changes in engines and fuel systems which had made the moon capture possible, something was now being done about their ability to defend themselves. It had taken Gutierrez five minutes to consider and approve the plan. *"Then we got ourselves a problem. My orders are t'prevent anybody else takin' 5023 Eris or learnin' its secrets, includin' our Russian friends. I'm here t'seize it or see it destroyed; it's up t'you folks down there. Y'all copy, General?"*

Dazzling against a star-flecked backdrop of black velvet, a space-suited figure made signals at him through the windshield: he should seal his helmet and gloves. Eichra Oren complied, helping Sam. Gutierrez shook his head and made stalling motions. "Not altogether, Admiral. Over."

The radio crackled. *"Horatio, like we say back in San Jacinto, it's time t'fish or get off the pot. Your earlier orders are rescinded. Your people will return t'Earth, to a hero's welcome an' substantial raises in pay and benefits, if they're willin' to—hold on a minute."*

Again the radio fell silent. Inside his helmet, Eichra Oren blinked in response to a sudden implant message. He put a hand on Gutierrez's shoulder. The general closed the end of his mike tube with his thumb. "What is it?"

"Mr. Thoggosh asks me to inform you that there are now

three armed fleets in orbit. An Admiral Hoong Liang is talking with him now, from *his* flagship, the *Dee Jen Djieh.*''

This time the name of the ship seemed vaguely familiar. Gutierrez had no more than nodded before Delacroix was back. *''Horatio, it's gettin' crowded out here. May be hard t'keep that promise—amnesty, a hero's welcome, pay an' benefits—shockin' how little store folks put in international treaties. I asked this Chinaman to explain himself, he said he's savin' his explanations for 'the Elders.' That make any sense to you? Over.''*

It should make sense to Delacroix or he should fire his Intelligence people. Gutierrez explained that the Elders were their nonhuman hosts. Outside, signals to seal his suit grew frantic or irritated, depending on how much respect he believed was being accorded his rank. Delacroix thanked him in ominous, gracious tones, replying that with two hostile fleets to watch now, he had ''chores.'' He'd recontact the general as soon as possible.

Gutierrez unhooked his carrier from the console, plugged it in inside his collar, and had just settled his helmet when another voice sounded in his ears: *''Greetings to the expeditionary party on 5023 Eris. This person is Admiral Hoong Liang of the Celestial Fleet of the People's Republic of China. Have I the honor to address General Horatio Gutierrez?''*

Unable to resist peering out for a sign of the latest arrival (he saw none), Gutierrez replied in the affirmative. Through repeaters set up in camp, thirty-odd other humans listened. At news of a coming fleet, they'd debated the course they should follow while Gutierrez's party was still underground. They'd failed to reach a conclusion, nor would they have been entitled to act if they had. He'd given no one except Sebastiano and Ortiz, who must pilot the other ships, his reasons for allowing the shuttles to be armed. They'd agreed as he'd known they would and now sat in the lefthand seats of their own craft, *John Galt* and *Geronimo*, awaiting orders.

"*I've explained to Mr. Thoggosh,*" Hoong replied, "*that my government, unlike certain others, is satisfied merely to keep the great ship you've discovered out of the exclusive hands of its potential enemies.*"

Gutierrez was suspicious. "You're saying you don't want it?"

"*Only the knowledge it represents.*" Hoong was amiable. "*I am confident that the Elders will someday share their own technology with us, whatever they find here. Perhaps they can be persuaded to establish regular trade with the Chinese People's Republic. In any event, as long as no nation has a monopoly on that knowledge and technology, we are content.*"

"Meaning what?" Both overhead observation windows chose that moment to pop from their frames, the round-cornered panes fielded by Eichra Oren as they drifted to the deck. This was the reason for insisting that they suit up inside the *Laika*, although no more than a heartbeat passed before the windows were replaced by mounting plates for the new weapons systems. Workmen trooped inboard and heavy cables soon extended into the command deck computers.

"*Meaning,*" replied Hoong, "*that the Elders and your expedition are free to do what they wish without interference. I am authorized to help guarantee that freedom, should you desire it.*" Admiral Hoong would be unaware that Mr. Thoggosh's mining equipment, basically electromagnetic cannons that fired plasma "torpedoes" of unthinkable brilliance and heat, was a better guarantee than any he could offer. It had failed to penetrate the secrets of 5023 Eris, but that didn't keep it from being installed on the shuttles and used as weaponry more effective than any Earth had yet developed.

"*I'm impressed*"—Mr. Thoggosh's voice was on the line—"*with your expression of self-interest, Admiral, so refreshing coming from a human. I daresay I haven't the faintest interest in trading with any Chinese People's Republic. I might, however, be persuaded to trade with Chinese people."*

Chinese *people*, Gutierrez noticed, not *the* Chinese People. He, too, was amazed by the admiral's offer, although he remained wary. China was a mystery to generations of Americans. In an odd way it was a reversal of her classical policy of closing out the world. The world, at least its leading Marxist nations, had closed her out. Nobody in America was supposed to know what went on there, any more than what was happening in Switzerland, Israel, or South Africa, all polities that refused—in terms measurable at times by body counts or megacuries—to join the United World Soviet.

"Mr. Thoggosh," Hoong replied, *I am humbled by your—"*

Whatever else he had to say was drowned in static as, through the shuttle window, Gutierrez watched a new star flare to life and wink out. No one was ever sure who fired it, but a missile of about a kilotonne's yield had been launched at the *Dee Jen Djieh*.

The instant its blip appeared on her radar, computer-controlled Gatling guns spewed tens of thousands of projectiles at it, failing to destroy it, but slewing it off course. When it ignited, it was thousands of meters off target. The organic canopy, where radiation rained upon it, turned blue-purple and returned to its original butter yellow again, absorbing furious energies and protecting the asteroid's tenants.

"Ortiz, Sebastiano, heads up!" Mindful to avoid the unnamed artificial moon, Gutierrez, the old fighter pilot's sizzle in his veins, ordered his ships aloft, noses aimed (the actual calculation was more complicated) at his estimate of the missile's launch point. Eichra Oren slammed into the righthand seat, assisting as if born to it. *Asteroids are wonderful*, Gutierrez thought, *for things they don't have, like significant gravity.* Shuddering, which made the overall effect better, *Laika* took off horizontally like the rockets in an old Flash Gordon serial.

The word *orbit* had been abused to describe the locus of Earth's fleets; the gravity of 5023 Eris was too negligible for that. The flotillas were disposed about the asteroid at 120-degree intervals, keeping an eye on both the surface and their rivals, but fuel—reaction mass, he reminded himself; those ships were fusion powered—was being expended to keep them there. He didn't know whether the missile had been Russian or American. His copilot informed him that the Elders didn't know; everyone had been rattled by that first shot. As his own ship clawed into the sky, he expected to be blasted any second and thanked somebody's lousy reaction time when it didn't happen.

"This is the Erisian Space Patrol," he told his mike and got a grin from Eichra Oren. "Alien fleets will withdraw to a distance of ten thousand klicks or be destroyed." He'd had no idea of tactics when he'd ordered the launch, just a pilot's reflexive need, with their base under attack, to get his planes off the deck. Might as well be hung for a sheep as a lamb.

Delacroix had the same preference. *John Reed* chose that moment to fire several missiles. Gutierrez suspected they were going to MIRV into dozens of smaller nuclear-tipped weapons. He couldn't tell whether they were aimed at the asteroid or the shuttlecraft. He nudged the attitude control to drop the nose and slew it to starboard, lined up crosshairs painted on the windshield, and slapped a panel duct-taped to his seat arm.

A ball of eye-searing brilliance flashed toward the American fleet at a respectable fraction of the speed of light, catching the missiles before they could disperse, enveloping them in a cloud of incandescent gas. As the wave front, attenuated by an intervening fifty kilometers, caught the *Laika*, he knew the critics were wrong to nitpick space operas for their battle scenes. Explosions in a vacuum are perfectly audible when they create their own temporary atmosphere. His ship buffeted by a man-made storm, he wrestled with the attitude controls and primary thrusters.

Whenever his makeshift sights brushed across the fleet again, he stood his thumb on the trigger panel and bore down. Distracted and confused, which was perfectly normal in combat, he never felt the blade sink into his neck until Eichra Oren leaped up to grapple with the assassin. Imprisoned by his seatbelt, unable to leave the controls in any event, the general could only watch—and listen—as whoever had attacked him caromed off the walls of the command deck with the Antarctican and his dog.

Sam couldn't use his teeth. Handicapped by his suit, he settled for springing from wherever he found himself and crashing into the struggling men, hitting Eichra Oren as often as the killer he fought. Eichra Oren, hampered by his clumsy NASA outfit, wasn't up to his martial best. It was all he could do to control the long, slim knife, still slippery with the general's blood.

The general's attention was elsewhere. So far, the intruding fleets had not engaged each other further, but were concentrating their energies on the three ancient but far from helpless shuttles. Gutierrez, one hand on the flight controls and the other on the firing panel, couldn't check to see how badly he was cut. He had to keep both eyes on the sky. Outside, another of Earth's ships exploded, spewing air and broken bodies.

He shook his head to clear it, which didn't produce any better results than it ever did. His own wound was beginning to hurt now. Air whistled from his punctured suit into a cabin that was only partly repressurized. The blade had glanced off the metal ring that formed the suit's collar and had entered, almost at right angles to the original thrust, driving between his collarbone and shoulder. Deep enough and he might lose a lung.

A flash of light somewhere behind him put an abrupt stop to the wrestling noises. Gutierrez risked a brief glance. Eichra Oren had his fusion pistol in his hand and a torn thigh pocket to go with it. Half the assassin's body lay against the deck. The lower half was missing. Where it had been was a waist-thick cauterized stump.

Gutierrez turned his attention to the battle again, just in time to sear another flock of missiles.

With effort, Eichra Oren pried the helmet from the attacker's head.

"Alvarez," Sam said. "I've been keeping an eye on him. What'll you bet he's Iron Butterfly, the one who probably summoned that fleet out there?"

"No bets," the general answered over his shoulder, "take a look at that!"

One of Gutierrez's automatic follow-up shots had fetched the *John Reed* a glancing blow on her starboard wingtip. He could see her now, along with two of her escorts, hypersonic aerospace planes larger than the shuttles, a fanciful design meant to carry a thousand passengers across the Pacific at many times the speed of sound. To his knowledge, the idea had been abandoned as pointlessly expensive and the craft never built. Now here they were, three of them—probably more out of sight—fitted as warships and carrying a swarm of smaller craft which they'd released just before the *John Reed* was hit. The explosion vaporized half a wing and set the flagship spinning like a badly balanced top about her yaw axis.

"They seem to have skimped on attitude controls," Sam observed as the flagship failed to slow and began breaking up with centrifugal stresses. Ignoring her, the smaller ships— lifeboats or landing craft, the general wasn't certain which— began jetting for the asteroid. Getting handier with the plasma cannon, he picked as many off as he could until the angles changed and the asteroid was within his field of fire. The defenders on the surface were about to be very busy.

Gutierrez had ordered Sebastiano's *John Galt* toward the five-ship Russian fleet. To him they were mere dots on radar, which, after a single multimissile salvo and a mass launch of their own small vessels, began to withdraw.

Sebastiano's cannon, spectacular even at this distance, batted the attack aside. The colonel's victory whoop—which he'd have expected sooner from Ortiz—rang in the general's ears, but Gutierrez didn't have the heart to reprimand him. One errant missile, still intact, seemed to impact without harm on the artificial moon.

Another volley, similar to that which had destroyed the *John Reed*, was less successful. The Russians had observed that the plasma weapons' speed far outstripped the reaction time of human or computerized gunners. They'd begun firing their Gatlings in the direction of Sebastiano's ship the instant they released their missiles. The resulting stream of projectiles was only partly effective at breaking up the ball of plasma streaking their way, but it saved the Russian flagship and the Banker with it. Damaged, the *Lavrenti Pavlovich Beria* withdrew at top velocity.

Gutierrez, one hand holding his ripped suit closed now, thought about picking up survivors from the *John Reed* but the remaining American ships beat him to it. He thought about examining his own wound, but pushed it out of his mind. Ortiz, following a longer assigned course toward the Chinese fleet, demanded attention. *"Don't look now, fellow space cadets,"* he remarked, *"but we're flanked!"*

The major was correct. Instead of firing missiles, the *Dee Jen Djieh* and three auxiliaries stooped on the asteroid like a bird of prey, releasing hundreds of smaller objects. The Yaqui officer described them as spacesuited figures who landed on the surface and disappeared. They seemed to have some easy means of penetrating the canopy. Mr. Thoggosh denied via implant having anything to do with it. His property was being invaded, he told Gutierrez through Eichra Oren, and he was sending security forces to deal with the intruders.

Before the general could give Eichra Oren a reply, light flared in the sky again. An unexpected interaction had occurred. Mr. Thoggosh's unbeinged orbital station, with its automated neutrino detector, was ablaze with dazzling white-hot thermonuclear fire. The nearby burst of the Russian atomic bomb had somehow ignited the little moonlet. The bizarre result was that a tiny artificial sun now brightened the sky of 5023 Eris.

XXIV
Sleeping Dragon

When Chinese forces began appearing near their camp, the Americans were treated to a surprise. Not one was wearing anything describable as a uniform. Their leader (and the rest as it turned out) spoke perfect colloquial English.

"Hi there!" A young Oriental in Levi's and a flannel shirt greeted Owen, the first person he encountered. "I'm Colonel Tai of the People's Republic Extra-Special Forces. Could you direct me to the officer in charge? I've orders from Admiral Hoong to place myself under his or her command. We're the cavalry arriving in the nick of time."

Sweating in the double-shadowed light of two suns, Owen looked to his companions, Danny and Tl*m*nch*l. To the sound of faraway gunfire, the two men were trying, with scorpionoid assistance, to defend this sector of the perimeter. They'd already had some sporadic shooting, nothing anyone would call a firefight, with Russian or American intruders (they weren't certain which) deeper in the forest. Whether this had produced any enemy casualties was something else they weren't sure of. They were unscathed.

Owen inspected the officer who, despite his clothing and a kerchief he'd tied to a branch, wore a large autopistol slung under one armpit in a black nylon harness and an even larger knife suspended handle-down under the other. "That'll be General Gutierrez," Owen told him, shifting the shotgun on his shoulder and lifting a broad thumb toward a canopy much brighter than when they'd first arrived. "He's busy right now and so are his seconds, Colonel Sebastiano and Major Ortiz. I'm Corporal Owen—" He gave Danny a nudge. "This is Lieutenant Gutierrez."

It was Danny's turn to blink, realizing that *he* was the officer in charge. "I suppose you'd better come with me, Colonel."

"Fine by me," the officer responded. He lifted fingers to his lips and whistled. Men and women in civilian clothing, more heavily armed than their leader and with a startling range of what were clearly personal weapons, began melting out of the forest. They formed a loose column to follow the two surprised and skeptical Americans to the camp.

The scorpionoid laid a foreclaw on Danny's shoulder and did his best to imitate a whisper with his voice simulator. "Why do you and Roger not take Colonel Tai with you. I will stay here with his people."

Danny saw the sense of it. "Good thinking, Tl*m*nch*l, but all alone?"

In the distance, a grenade *crumped*. Chitin-armored manipulators rattled on Tl*m*nch*l's synthesizer where it hung beside his pistol. "No, Lieutenant, my people are scattered through these woods and are alert. We'll encircle them, should this prove to be a trick. Show the colonel your camp, I'll wait here."

"Okay." Danny turned to the young officer. "Colonel, I can't bring your whole unit back with me. If they'll wait here with Tl*m*nch*l, we can go see Mr. Empleado or Pin—I mean, Major Ortega y Pena."

Tai glanced at Tl*m*nch*l as if he were used to seeing aliens every day. "Okay, Lieutenant. One question: what do you want done with these?"

At a gesture, several troops dragged half a dozen figures forward, arms bound behind them, and threw them at

Danny's feet. It was less cruel than it might have been at full gravity. Danny looked down at two Russian *spetznatz* officers in battle dress and four bruised and disgruntled ASSR Marines.

"—estimates from my experts that our artificial sun will be short lived, merely lasting a couple of thousand years. They're readjusting the temperature and humidity as we speak."

At camp, Mr. Thoggosh was more in charge than anyone else. He'd returned with the general from the dig, but had decided to direct his own defenses from here, drinking beer through a plastic tube in his protective suit. Sporadic, faraway gunfire could still be heard as the Chinese, the expeditionaries, and the party of the Elders continued mopping up invaders.

"I'm impressed, Colonel Tai." the Proprietor admitted once a kettle had been set on the fire for tea. "We and our allies—with individuals from the ASSR expedition—welcome your support with gratitude. We nautiloids are amateurs in a field in which humans are the acknowledged experts."

Adjusting his weapons harness, the colonel settled by the fire despite the warmth overhead. He glanced around at the tents and other evidence of people roughing it on a terraformed asteroid. "And that is?"

"War, my dear Colonel. We haven't fought one in thousands of millennia. And in this particular battle, I'm afraid, nobody has the proper equipment or is altogether certain what to do. It was pure good fortune that our canopy was 'smart' enough to filter out radiation from atomic weapons. Which reminds me—would you mind telling me how you got through it?"

"I'm curious about that, myself." Still in his spacesuit, Gutierrez strode into camp with Sam and Eichra Oren. Toya rose from the fire to stand at the latter's side. Rosalind, who'd started to get up, sat down again. Danny suspected that Eichra Oren was about to have trouble. "Before anybody asks, the shooting's stopped, at least for now. Looks like the Russians and Americans have withdrawn and are headed back to Earth amidst ugly muttering from the Banker. Ortiz and Sebastiano are still upstairs patrolling, backed by Admiral Hoong. My ship's refueling so I can relieve them."

The man looked drawn and pale to his son and held his head at an angle. Perhaps only Danny understood that there was more to it than refueling or his father would have stayed with his ship. The Chinese fleet was out there which meant that, having long avoided it, the rest of the expedition would now be forced to choose sides as the pilots had. It was a situation unlike any they'd faced before. In Danny's mind were old movies he'd seen about West Point on the eve of the War Between the States.

"Enzymes," replied Colonel Tai. "Your first reports were analyzed and, well, passed on, both to Russian and Chinese intelligence. I believe we arrived at the solution first, but . . ."

Gutierrez laughed. "Your secrets are as volatile as everybody else's?"

The colonel grimaced. "In any event, spray-application opened the canopy and closed it so that little air was lost. You've seen our prisoners?" He indicated the Russians and Americans, squatting in a row against one of the modules removed from the shuttles to make room for fuel. "We captured these Marines on the ground having killed many of their comrades, but the Russians were trapped halfway through the canopy like flies in amber. These are the survivors. Their aerosol was too dilute."

"Russian quality control." Gutierrez shook his head. "Very well, Colonel, what do you intend doing now?"

"Whatever you ask, sir, consistent with my nation's interests. I'm to assist under your orders. This group's one of twenty-three of which I'm in command. Altogether we are five hundred twenty-nine." He tapped an earpiece he was wearing. "I'm told we now have a great many more prisoners, too."

The firing did seem to be tapering off. The general whistled at the prospect of his command increasing more than tenfold. "Thanks, Colonel, I'll get back to you. If you'll excuse me . . ." He turned to Danny. "Lieutenant, have the company fall in, those not engaged in essential tasks."

"Sir!" Danny snapped a salute and began gathering the shuttle crews together. Perhaps the others had anticipated what was about to happen; the task was accomplished in a few minutes.

It was obvious Mr. Thoggosh was satisfied. Rounding up personnel, Danny overheard him tell Eichra Oren, without benefit of their implants, that it was a sign "these organisms" were learning to think for themselves. "Despite Aelbraugh Pritsch's contrary urging," he'd told the Antarctican, "I intend to refrain from offering advice. As I informed my assistant, if they can learn to do the right thing, perhaps bird-beings might learn to relax a little." Eichra Oren had glanced at Toya and chuckled. Sam had said something about Hell freezing over. Danny assumed the message was meant for American ears although he didn't know why he'd been chosen to hear it. He'd pass it along to his father. The assembled company were asked to sit on the ground.

"So far," the general told his people, "events haven't left us much time for choices. The arrival of three fleets from Earth was a surprise even to the Elders, and we were fired on without warning. All we've done is defend ourselves. It may take some fancy legal work, but if anybody's interested, I'm willing to bet the offer from Admiral Delacroix is still open, and that the Banker will be willing to talk a deal, as well. Now that we've bought the time, we all have thinking to do."

Gutierrez reminded his fellow humans of everything that had happened here. On one hand, he pointed out, there were the Elders who, in their gruff, perplexing manner, had befriended them. They owed their lives many times over to these odd beings from a parallel reality. On the other hand, there were the governments of their own planet, made up of human beings like themselves. Did the expeditionaries owe them any special loyalty?

"Loyalty," Rosalind spoke aloud, yet almost as if she were speaking to herself, "is supposed to be a two-way street."

"Excellent point," answered the Russian agriculturalist, Valerian. "Have these institutions ever done anything but exploit those of whom they demand loyalty—and in our case, betray and abandon us?"

"General Gutierrez, I demand that you put a stop to these disgusting amateur individualistics!" It was Empleado. "Our duty is clear! This talk is treason, not just to our government but humanity itself!"

"Hang it in your ear, KGB cockroach!" Danny watched his father avoid seeing who'd said that. Time passed before other replies, mostly obscene, tapered off. As his father continued, Danny found that his own choice wasn't that hard. It was true that, if he sided with the Elders, he might never see his family—mother, brothers, sisters—again. His father had to be aware of that and of the fact that the government might take his defection out on his wife and children. Danny also knew that this didn't make them different from anyone else here.

Although he couldn't say why, he felt making the right choice was the best help he could give his family. He also knew that his father faced other problems. Despite remarks that represented nothing less than the truth, he wouldn't want, even by implication, to make choices for others. Wasn't the point of this situation the right and necessity to do that for oneself? This meant that Danny should wait until the last minute before declaring himself, so as not to tip the balance. As it was, the others seemed to be having more difficulty than their general and his son.

"I worry most," Gutierrez told them, "that after all

we've been through, we'll find ourselves peering at each other over gunsights." He looked at his audience, most carrying weapons as they had since the initial misunderstanding with the Elders. "At the same time, you can bet the Banker's preoccupied with his own great fear that we might use Predecessor technology to defend ourselves. He may not know it, but his concern is groundless."

They gave him a disappointed groan. Many who hadn't helped explore below had been harboring hopes of a miracle.

"Sorry, but it'll be years before we understand what 5023 Eris is capable of, let alone take advantage of it. Of course that hasn't stopped Nikola Deshovich from trying to prevent it. What he didn't count on was that, even with Predecessors' systems still inactive, we're far from helpless."

"What do you mean, General?" the geologist Guillermo interrupted. "I thought we were surrounded."

Gutierrez sighed. "Hector, there's a lesson here if we're smart enough. At home we delegate personal defense to the authorities."

"So scum—" Danny was unable to help himself—"like Deshovich run things."

His father shrugged. "Fair enough. By contrast, the nautiloids are accustomed to personal weaponry." From a pocket, he pulled the 9m/m pistol he'd carried since finding it on Richardson's body. "To tell the truth, I've gotten used to it myself. Eichra Oren's little hypervelocity steam gun typifies the potency of arms available to the Elders. The point is that each of these beings controls his own destiny."

Ortega y Pena snorted. "Small arms against nuclear weapons?"

"Excuse me, Horatio, I didn't intend to interrupt." Mr. Thoggosh drew himself toward the group. "You mentioned a lesson to be learned. This Banker of yours didn't want to destroy his enemies so much as steal what belongs to them, is that correct?"

"Not *my* Banker, Mr. Thoggosh. Otherwise, you're right."

"Still, his purpose would be lost in destroying what he wants to seize."

'The botanist nodded. "Which is why he withdrew for the present. A wise barbarian loots *before* he burns. The one way he could do that was to come down and fight at a level where small arms are effective. And he lost."

"For the time being, Federico, as you say," the general answered. "The nukes he brought were an empty threat. His manpower, drawn from World Soviet 'peacekeeping' forces, came expecting to assault undefended territory." He indicated the prisoners. "Doctrine gave them no preparation for an armed population. Makes for an effective defense policy, doesn't it? But at a price no government is willing to pay—"

"Limitations on its own power," Ortega y Pena offered, "set by the same armed population."

Mr. Thoggosh chuckled. "They *are* beginning to learn, Horatio."

"On Earth, too," declared Colonel Tai. "Before we ran into Corporal Owen, we, well, *asked* our friends over there some leading questions."

Toya gasped. "You tortured them?"

Tai laughed. "Didn't have to—Pulaski, is it? They gave themselves mental hernias thinking up information to swap for their lives. Some would have gone home for more if we'd let them, and come back to give it to us. Point is, there are scattered uprisings all over Earth. The effort to seize this asteroid exhausted the resources of Russia and America, weakened both governments, and deprived their leaders of any remaining credibility."

"So it's over."

"Not sure I'd go that far, General. The Banker survived the battle. Doubtless he'll continue to be the first-class nuisance he's always been."

"And what will your people do?"

"After things are squared away here, you mean? Well, some of us are preparing to return to Earth. If your people are concerned about events at home or worried about their families, they're free to return with us if they wish—and if you permit, of course.''

''I appreciate the courtesy, but anybody can go back who wants to—including prisoners. Won't that make a crowded trip back for you, though?''

''Not me, General. Many of us have elected to remain. After all, there's so much to be learned from the Elders.''

''All right, welcome to 5023 Eris, then. Danny, dismiss the company and let them do their own thinking. Rosalind, can I see you a moment? I've got a paying customer for you—me.''

XXV
Epilogue: Unfinished Business

Eichra Oren was sweating.

An artificial sun burned through the canopy, sharpening the shadows without raising temperatures. New friends and old enemies had departed for mankind's homeworld hours ago. Order was being restored to the motley communities of 5023 Eris.

By anybody's estimate, his professional tasks were over with. Now he steeled himself to attend to personal business. It was necessary, he told himself, yet something he'd dreaded for weeks. His relationship with Toya, as artificial as the second sun shining overhead, had been imposed on him. From the first it had troubled his sense of ethics. The simple fact was that he found her about as unattractive as a human being could be. He felt guilty, but there was nothing he could do to hide it from himself, nor, knowing what he did of sapient psychology, would he have tried.

Just to make things complicated, he was more than interested in Rosalind. She was everything Toya could never be, graceful, beautiful, confident, even mysterious. The one similarity between the two women was their intelligence. Rosalind was unafraid of hers and used it to accomplish things in a real world, rather than as a refuge. Before he could do anything about that, however, he had a debt to pay. It was possible that it might spoil whatever chance he had with Rosalind, but as a man and as a debt assessor, he couldn't afford to abdicate. He must tell Toya the truth about his assignment from Mr. Thoggosh. Try as he might, in his 529 years of experience, he couldn't think of anything he'd looked forward to less.

After searching the world over—his legs ached from being folded under him in the electrostat he'd requisitioned for the purpose—he found her near the yawning triangular entrance to the interior. A canvas awning had been put up on poles to protect its occupants from what weather the asteroid had to offer. Beneath it, a large table had been built from newly sawn logs.

"Did you have a chance to talk with Colonel Tai about his background?" she was asking her companion. "I hear that the Chinese who came here are the result of endless batteries of personality tests as children and underwent decades of isolation and cold-blooded conditioning."

There had already been another brief subsurface excursion. Toya was examining Predecessor artifacts of a technical nature, spread out on the table before her. Nearby lay solvents, soap and water, brushes of various sizes and stiffness. Bending over the table beside her, the machinist Owen was attempting to identify each of the pieces as it was cleaned off.

"What kind of training? Hello, Eichra Oren."

The Antarctican nodded back. Owen was fresh shaven, wearing what Eichra Oren was certain had been a clean uniform. He was shocked at this miraculous transformation. He hadn't seen an ironed uniform during his entire acquaintance with his fellow human beings on the asteroid, and Owen was the last individual he'd have expected to be wearing one. Sharp creases and pocket folds were still visible, although he and Toya were covered, head to toe, with several eons' accumulation of dust and dirt. It was clear to any observer that they were having the time of their lives.

"Hello, Eichra Oren," Toya echoed and went on. "Well, some subjects he mentioned were 'Elementary Practical Jokes,' 'Intermediate Intransigence,' 'Advanced Profanity,' and 'Postgraduate Greed.'"

"All intended," Eichra Oren told them, "to mimic the rugged individualism they feel was once characteristic of Americans and made you a great people. You began to decline—Tai's words, although I agree—when 'team play' and other forms of soft collectivism became the order of the day. 'Ask not what your country can do for you,' et cetera, et cetera, et cetera."

"You're saying it was Wall Street and Madison Avenue types who ruined us," Owen asked, "rather than Marxists?"

"I'm saying—Colonel Tai is—that Marxism would have been laughed out of existence without Wall Street and Madison Avenue doing its advance work. However, the kind of rugged individual the Chinese most admire and try to emulate isn't Rambo or John Wayne, although it's true that warriors are useful and comforting to have around, but the technically oriented 'nerd.'"

Toya started. Owen repeated, "Nerd?"

"Sure. Tai pointed out that the Japanese, to name a bad example, lost their technological and economic lead over that very issue. Not once during the twentieth or twenty-first centuries has that country suffered from mischievous hacking nor lost a single person-hour to a domestic computer virus."

"This is bad?" There was a twinkle in Owen's eye.

"The Chinese think it's bad for any culture. Like the lack of crime in England—because they haven't got the gumption for it—the Japanese lack the requisite individualism for such pranks. It's beaten out of them at an early age, along with any real creativity, by their conformist schoolmates."

Owen nodded. "Therefore they lacked resources—the mental capital—for maintaining their otherwise impressive mid twentieth-century gains."

"That's about it. The Chinese decided to close their own potential 'nerd gap.' They built whole villages, high in the mountains or deep in the deserts, where individualism was practiced like a foreign language. It was their hope that someday their experimental subjects could leave the villages to spread that language among the rest of the people."

Toya shook her head. "But instead they risked everything to preserve the international balance of power? That doesn't make much sense."

Eichra Oren shrugged. "The whole effort would be for nothing if the Russians or Americans acquired exclusive control of an overwhelmingly advanced technology." He cleared his throat. "Pardon me for changing the subject, Roger, but I need to speak with Toya, if you don't mind."

Before Owen could speak, Toya astonished them both. She blinked and looked at Eichra Oren. "I know why you're here and we don't have to make a big deal of it. There isn't anything we can't say in front of Roger."

Owen pointed a stubby finger at his own chest, mouthing the word *moi*?

Toya ignored him and continued speaking to the Antarctican. "I've been dreading this moment, having to tell you the truth, for weeks. I was assigned, against my will, by General Gutierrez and Arthur Empleado, to distract you and learn the Elders' secrets. I want to make it clear that I have nothing against you. I enjoyed what happened and I hope you did, too. It didn't just make me feel like a woman, it made me feel like a full-fledged human being for the first time in my life. I'll always be grateful to you for that. But let's be realistic. I had my orders from the KGB, and I'll bet you had yours, too, from Mr. Thoggosh.''

Eichra Oren felt like imitating Owen, but she didn't give him time.

''Now I have my own interest.'' He knew that she meant something other than intellectual interests. Her gaze directed itself at the overweight, grease-covered machinist standing next to her. ''And from the way you look at Dr. Nguyen and the way she looks at you, I'd guess that you have yours, as well. Over the past weeks, I've learned to value you as a colleague and friend, Eichra Oren. Why can't we just leave it at that?''

Heretofore, Owen had been a dedicated bachelor, the expedition character. The lives of the Americans often depended on his ability to fabricate whatever they needed. Laying a grimy hand on Toya's, he looked up from his work and grinned man-to-man at the assessor. Something about that grin told Eichra Oren he was more than he appeared to be. Not knowing what else to do, Eichra Oren grinned back, nodded at Toya, left the pair to their archaeological research, and stumped back the way he'd come to his waiting aerocraft.

To his surprise he found anger bubbling up inside him and knew he had some thinking to do before he could call his mind his own again. It wasn't that he'd wanted the girl. She was right. His interests, like hers, lay elsewhere. Yet his ego felt bruised by rejection and he was dismayed to discover such a childish reaction lurking within him. It was another phenomenon he felt reluctant to tell his mother about. He knew from experience that this was a danger sign. He'd never been anything resembling a mother's boy. Eneri Relda, an active individual with ''interests'' of her own, would never have permitted it. but she was also a person of acute judgment who'd lived fifteen thousand years. He valued her advice even when receiving it was painful or embarrassing.

By the time he reached his aerocraft, he'd had time to consider further and realized, with gratification, what had happened. As usual, the Elders' ancient *p'Nan* philosophy was proven correct. On the Forge of Adversity, Toya had transformed herself into her own person, self-confident and autonomous. And almost pretty, in a way, now that he came to think of it. It pleased him to believe he might have had something to do with the change.

Relieved—and free—he went to look for Rosalind.